T0152383

# The Man
# Who Killed
# Durruti

First published in Great Britain in 2005
by Read and Noir, an imprint of ChristieBooks
PO Box 35
Hastings, East Sussex
TN34 2UX
christie@btclick.com

Distributed in the UK by Central Books Ltd
99 Wallis Road, London E9 5LN
orders@centralbooks.com

ISBN   1-873976-26-7

British Library Cataloguing in Publication Data.
A catalogue record for this book is available from the British Library

Originally published in Spanish as *El Hombre Que Mató A Durruti*

The author's rights have been asserted

*Signed copies and sets of postcards of the original illustrations are
available from Richard Warren at rwarren99@yahoo.com*

# The Man
# Who Killed
# Durruti

by
## Pedro de Paz

*Winner of the 2003 José Saramago
International Short Novel Award*

Translated by Paul Sharkey
Postscript by Stuart Christie
Illustrations by Richard Warren

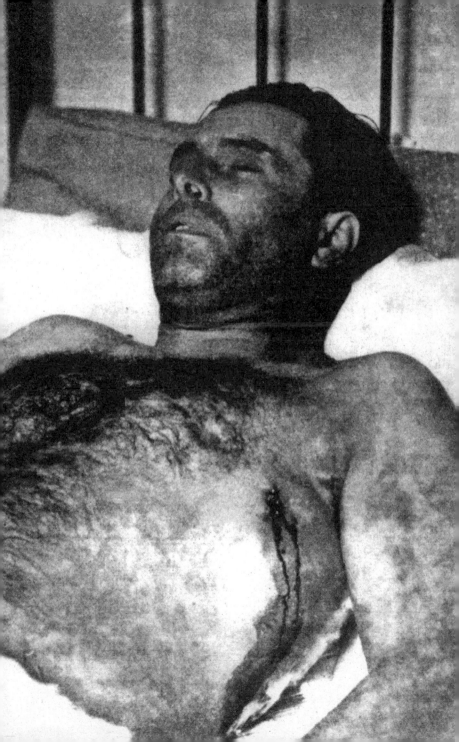

THE GLOOMY ROOM reeked of dampness and fear. Its location in the basement, the *checa*, of the building in the Calle de Fomento, and the austere furnishings — a plain wooden table, two chairs, one at each side and a desk in one corner — confirmed that it was in fact an interrogation room. All of Madrid knew what went on at the Fomento *checa*. Merely finding oneself there, voluntarily or otherwise, struck fear even into the bravest man. The room contained one man, seated on one of the chairs, toying nervously with the *miliciano's* cap he held in his hands. He was waiting, but for what he did not know. A cold sweat trickled down his back and the waiting made him feel more and more uncomfortable with every passing moment. Eventually, the door opened and in stepped two men dressed in officers' uniforms. Without a word, they began leafing through papers they brought with them in a leather briefcase. From time to time, they would raise their eyes to observe this fellow before returning to the documents. One of them was taller than the other, nearer forty rather than thirty, with a dour weather-beaten face and tiny, grey, piercing eyes. His movements and bearing suggested a certain authority. The other man was younger, his age indeterminate but around the mid-twenties. He appeared more affable with a less harsh expression, but his attitude and, above all, the deference he showed towards his colleague suggested he was there purely as an assistant. Finally, the older officer closed the briefcase, setting it on the table and turned to the man seated there.

"Name?"

The man jumped to attention before the officer.

"Julio Graves. At your orders, Major."

"At ease, Graves," the senior officer replied. "Please be seated."

The man's younger colleague took a seat in a corner of the room, taking notes.

"I am Major Fernández Durán and this is Lieutenant Alcázar," the major said, gesturing towards the younger man. "Do you know why you are here?"

"No, Major," Graves replied, rather diffidently. "I was merely ordered to come here."

Fernández Durán sat down, his back to the door, facing Graves, watching him closely. A few moments later, he slowly removed some papers from his briefcase, spread them out on the table and ran a barely interested eye over them, as if he knew the contents by heart. Finally, he spoke to Graves.

"According to documents in our possession," Fernández Durán stated, pointing to the papers laid out on the table, "until recently you were comandante Durruti's driver. Is that correct?"

Graves, stricken with fear, appeared none too sure whether the right answer — the expected answer — was yes or no. He finally decided to tell the truth. After all, he had nothing to hide.

"Yes, sir," Graves replied.

"And that you were on duty on the day that Durruti was struck by the bullet that ended his life on 19 November last," Major Fernández Durán pressed him.

"Yes, sir, that is correct."

"Tell us what happened that day. I know that it has been almost two months now but try to stick to the facts as best you can. And include as much detail as you can call to mind."

The nervous Graves took a deep breath. He still had no idea why he had been sent for and this place was doing little to dispel his misgivings.

"That morning we were at the headquarters of the Durruti Column in the Calle Miguel Ángel." Julio Graves stared into the distance, trying to recall the events of that day. "I was preparing the car because we were off on a reconnaissance trip, if I remember correctly. Somebody arrived at the headquarters and spoke with Durruti for a few minutes. I remember as they were chatting Durruti looked particularly irritated and was gesticulating and making lots of extravagant gestures. As soon as this conversation ended, Durruti came to tell me that we would be leaving immediately for the University City. We climbed into the car and headed in that direction.

"Can you remember the name of the person who spoke with Durruti?" Fernández Durán interjected.

"No, Major, but I do know it was someone from the column. I had seen him on several occasions, but, as to his name, I don't know.

"Who got into the car?"

"Sergeant Manzana accompanied commandante Durruti, as usual — and myself, sir."

"Continue," signalled Fernández Durán.

"We arrived at the Plaza de Cuatro Caminos and I sped down the Avenida de Pablo Iglesias. We passed by a few small houses at the end of the avenue before taking a right turn. I remember that it was a very fine day. It came as a shock to me to think that November was upon us already. Arriving at a junction, we spotted a group of *milicianos* who appeared to be coming to meet us. Durruti suspected that these lads were bent on abandoning the front and he ordered me to stop the car. Damned if I didn't, Major. We were in a firing zone. Moorish troops occupying the Clinical Hospital and overlooking the area were sniping at everything that moved. We could hear nothing but shooting on every side. To be on the safe side, I parked the car on the corner of one of the small hotels in the area. Durruti and Manzana climbed out of the car and went over to the *milicianos*, asking where they were going. Caught red-handed, the soldiers did not know how to answer. Durruti gave them a tongue-lashing and ordered them back to their posts.

"Precisely where along the way was that stop made?" pressed Fernández Durán.

"I couldn't say for certain, Major," replied Graves. "As I said, we drove down the Avenida de Pablo Iglesias then turned left down a curving street lined with small hotels. I think it was the Avenida del Valle, but I am not certain about that. It was at the end of that street that we took a right turn, pulling up just beyond.

"And did you get out of the vehicle?" Fernández Durán pressed again.

"No sir. I was at the wheel and kept the engine running, waiting for them to get back in so that we could get to safety as soon as possible. As I have told you, the area was being swept by enemy gunfire."

"And what happened after that?"

"The soldiers bawled out by Durruti tucked their tails between their legs and turned back, Major. Durruti and Sergeant Manzana made their way back towards the car. We were facing the Clinical Hospital and the

4

rebels were still shooting. Several bullets whistled close by. Very close, Major. It was as if the Moors had realised we were there and — it being an easy target — had decided to let fly at the car. Behind me I heard Durruti opening the rear door of the car when a shot rang out. Durruti collapsed and fell to the ground, his chest covered with blood. I jumped out of the car and, together with Manzana, placed him on the back seat. I did a U-turn with the car and headed full speed for the hospital at the Hotel Ritz. On arrival we were seen by Doctor Santamaría, the column physician, and Durruti was quickly taken to the operating theatres in the hotel basement. Manzana and I returned to headquarters to await news or further instructions. That night we went back to the Hotel Ritz. Durruti was very poorly and had lost consciousness. Doctor Santamaría told us that the outlook was very poor, that the wound was very serious and that he could not say if he would last the night." Julio Graves's eyes misted over and his voice broke. "He didn't, sir. Never made it. He died that very morning."

Graves dropped his eyes to the cap he held in his hands and said no more. Fernández Durán allowed Julio Graves a few moments to compose himself. Upset, Graves raised his eyes and cleared his throat. Fernández Durán resumed his questioning as if nothing had happened in order to spare the fellow further upset.

"Was anyone else hurt in the incident?"

"No, sir. Durruti was the only one wounded."

"And in your view, Graves, what happened?"

"Those damned fascists, sir. The rebels had overrun the hospital and were firing in every direction. Somebody went to sleep that night not realising just how much damage he had done. Whoever fired that shot might not have aimed it and fired at random, but that single shot killed one of the finest men I ever met."

"That's fine, Graves. Is there anything that you would like to add?"

"No, Major."

"You may go."

Graves stood up and walked to the door. Just as he was about to step outside, he paused for a moment, hesitated for a tenth of a second as if about to add something and finally left, shutting the door behind him, leaving the officers behind in the room.

Fernández Durán sat, staring straight ahead, not saying a word. Then he turned to his assistant.

"What do you make of that, Lieutenant?"

"Nothing special, Major," Alcázar replied. He added a few more details of which we were unaware, but essentially the facts tally with those in the reports already available to us."

"Were you able to locate all of the names on the list I gave you, Alcázar?" inquired Fernandez Durán.

"Yes, sir," replied Alcázar as he stood up and moved closer to Fernández Durán. "Except for the *milicianos* Durruti bawled out. I haven't been able to trace them. But I have asked Captain Angulo from the Del Rosal Column to drop by."

"And who might this Captain Angulo be, Alcázar?" asked a curious Fernández Durán. "He is not on the list I gave you. Nor is he named as an eye-witness in any of our reports."

"He wasn't a witness, Major." Alcázar explained. "When I was trying to trace the *milicianos* I was told that Captain Angulo was the officer commanding the *agrupación* to which they were attached and I was told, too, that he has first hand knowledge of what happened, as reported to him by his men. So I took the liberty of asking him to come by.

"Good work, Alcázar."

Alcázar hesitated for a moment. Finally he decided to put to the major a question that had been niggling him.

"Permission to speak, Major?"

"Go ahead, Lieutenant."

"Sir, I was surprised that the list you handed me was so short. According to our reports — and indeed the word on the streets — there were more witnesses who claimed to have been present and to have seen what happened."

"Alcázar, I am already aware, from the reports and from various affidavits, that there were more witnesses. I might even say, too many. If we accept the validity of the statements from everybody who says he saw the whole thing, the area must have been as crowded as the Plaza de las Ventas at five in the afternoon on bullfight day. With an event of this importance, everybody wants his day in the limelight. But over the days we have spent examining those reports handed to us, you yourself noticed that many accounts differed one from another and there were lots of inconsistencies with the statements taken. After detailed scrutiny of the reports and in accordance with my findings, I have confined myself to summoning those consistently and verifiably present and who must, beyond the shadow of a doubt, have seen what happened There will be plenty of time to summon further persons should we see fit to do so, but for the time being, I see no need until we have questioned all those whom we have summoned and discover if we are in a position to arrive at a conclusion. Who do we have left to question today, Lieutenant?"

"Everybody on the list has appointments for today, except for Sergeant Manzana who was away on the Aragón front commanding the Durruti Column and who won't return to Madrid until tomorrow afternoon. The other interviewees are waiting in the adjoining office. Doctor Santamaría has not arrived yet, but he did say that he would attend today."

"Good. Show the next one in."

"Yes, Major."

Alcázar left the room while Fernández Durán leafed through the reports he held in his hands. As Lieutenant Alcázar had stated, Julio Graves's account had tallied closely with the official version, the version that was spreading by word of mouth through official offices and which everyone accepted as trustworthy. There was nothing to hint at anything untoward in the entire matter. Just another casualty of war. Even so, he had accepted this curious assignment. Perhaps it was the sixth sense that he had developed over many years as a policeman. That sense — acquired over many years in the business — telling him that something was just not right here. Ever since he had familiarised himself with the details of the case, there had been certain aspects not to Fernández Durán's liking. Such as his own assignment, to look no further than that. Even though it involved the death of an outstanding militia commander and an outstanding figure in the fight against the rebel military, even though it represented an incalculable loss, it was still just another loss on front-line service. To some extent, he found it truly odd that he had been assigned to lead an investigation into the matter. He remembered how, back in early January 1937, while he was serving in Barcelona, he had taken a phone call one day from one of his superiors informing him that his presence had been requested at an important meeting scheduled to take place shortly. A meeting that would be attended by leading members of the republican government. It was Fernández Durán's belief that his work would be confined to the routine surveillance and escort duties to which he had been assigned and in which he was engaged at the time, but his superior quickly disabused him of that. The explanation brooked no challenge. They had explicitly requested him to attend and not in an escort capacity. Doubtless on the basis of his record of police service and the reputation he had deservedly acquired in the days prior to the civil war for his policeman's intuition and his fine record in solving cases routinely assigned to him, a panel had picked him out to mount an investigation of the circumstances surrounding the death of comandante Buenaventura Durruti. And he was under strict instructions to conduct that investigation with the utmost confidentiality, reporting solely and exclusively to that panel. To begin with, he was surprised by the commission and above all the conditions under which it was to be conducted, but when he had an interview with the members of the panel a few days after that in order to clarify a few details, his initial surprise evaporated when he found that those present included high-ranking officials of the republican government who had maintained a firm and genuine friendship with the deceased. And he had come away from that meeting with the firm conviction that this was not so much an official assignment as rather a semi-official one in which personal interests seemed to be at stake. At that meeting he had been handed what little documentation there was on the matter and, in order to help him carry out his assignment he was assigned as his assistant a Lieutenant Alcázar. *El sabueso* (Bloodhound) as he was nicknamed. A man of rather limited education, though he could read and write well enough, something of which not everybody in these days could boast, but endowed with an outstanding, sharp intellect, proven honesty and confidentiality and enjoying great social charm and a startling facility for pulling any assignment off, even in the times of scarcity attributable to the war; anything from running a specific individual to ground, no matter how hard, to a crate of French champagne. Fernández Durán and Alcázar spent days combing through archives, studying statements and reports, collating all the information they could find and finally coming to the conclusion that the most solid leads were to be found in the Spanish capital, the scene of the events. They applied for leave to travel to Madrid in order to pursue their investigation. They had arrived in Madrid three days ago and in record time, thanks to Alcázar's diligent arrangements — God alone knew whom he had had to make promises to, tip, fawn over or bribe (Fernández Durán preferred not to know) — they had discovered the whereabouts of Durruti's driver, as well as of the rest of the alleged witnesses whose statements Fernández Durán deemed vital if he was to get to the bottom of this matter.

The door to the room opened, breaking his train of thought and admitting Alcázar followed by a man dressed in the militiaman's typical blue overalls. Alcázar closed the door once the man was inside and stepped over to the same corner he had occupied during the questioning of Julio Graves, to resume his note-taking. He never said a word but his movements betrayed a mixture of wariness and resignation. In spite of the zeal he had displayed in the performance of his duties, Alcázar regarded the whole affair as a waste of time. It was all too plain to him what had happened in the matter of Durruti's death. The official version as set out in the report was feasible, correct and it was not worth the trouble of looking for twists and turns where there were none and in fact he had said as much to Fernández Durán in conversations prior to these interrogations. Even so, Fernández Durán had insisted on proceeding with the mission assigned to them by the most efficient and comprehensive means possible.

The man who had come in with Alcázar remained standing to attention. He was a pitiful sight to behold. Grimy, slovenly and most likely famished, his unshaven face bore the marks of weeks of unrelieved fighting. It was almost a certainty that he had been pulled away from front-line service to attend this interview. Fernández Durán looked him over with a mixture of compassion and respect. Not so much for this fellow as for all who were doubtless in the same position just then.

"Take a seat, please," said Fernández Durán deferentially, moved at the sight of this *miliciano*.

The man complied without a word, settling himself on the chair where only moments before Julio Graves had been sitting. The look in his eye mirrored a certain expectancy, this situation being so queer. Fernández Durán seated himself facing the man.

"Your name, comrade?" asked Fernández Durán cordially.

"My name is Antonio Bonilla," pausing. "Am I under arrest, Major?"

"Not at all. You're here to provide answers to a few questions," replied Fernández Durán. "What is your posting, comrade Bonilla?"

"I'm with the Durruti Column, Major," Bonilla responded. His tone was straightforward and genial. "We arrived in Madrid a little over two months ago on 15 November, from the Aragon front. No sooner had we arrived than we were dispatched to the University City because, it seems, there was a lot of action down there. You can say that again! It was a slaughterhouse, you know? At least half of our men perished within five days."

"Tell me what happened on 19 November last," Fernández Durán asked.

Bonilla stared at him with a mixture of scepticism and fear etched in his eyes.

"What do you mean, *mi comandante*?"

"You know perfectly well what I am referring to. Begin at the beginning, please. What happened that day?"

Bonilla hesitated. Despite the initial easy-going, affable attitude, Fernández Durán was looking at him somewhat severely. Bonilla swallowed some saliva and started to speak.

"As I said, Major, we were assigned to the University City. We had taken cover in a number of chalets near the Clinical Hospital. We could see the enemy framed in the hospital's windows and they could see us. From time to time we exchanged a few shots, but, apart from that, the area was pretty quiet. On the night of the 18th a captain of the Del Rosal Column's dynamiters came over and told us that he had discovered that overnight the rebel forces had pulled out of the hospital via an underground passage linking the hospital to the Casa de Velázquez, to withdraw to their own lines and get fresh ammunition and that we would capitalise on that

that night to capture the hospital when the rebels withdrew. We decided that at four o'clock in the morning we would open up on the hospital windows and that if there was no reply from the enemy, that would indicate that the building was clear and we would rush it. We did just that at daybreak that day, the 19th, and when there was no return fire, we rushed the hospital, leaving behind a sniper party, of which I was one, to cover our retreat, should we have to make one. They gained entry without any difficulty. You should have seen the celebrations, Major! In next to no time they could be heard singing 'The Internationale' at the top of their lungs from the flat roof of the building. Except that they were singing the proper lyrics, Major, the anarchist lyrics. Within a short while we picked up the sound of raised voices and shooting. The rebels had returned via the underground passage, and, finding the hospital occupied, shooting broke out inside the hospital proper, as every floor was fought over. It was a real shindig, Major. Little by little, our troops were withdrawing from the hospital and making their way back to where we were. As they drew level they mentioned that they were withdrawing on the express orders and under the command of one of the captains with the Del Rosal Column and it occurred to me that our own commander, Durruti, should be told how things stood and further instructions requested of him."

Bonilla paused here and appeared to have concluded his account. It was all too obvious that he had no desire to go any further along the road Fernández Durán was hoping for and had digressed as much as he could.

"I'm not looking for war dispatches from that day, Bonilla," said Fernández Durán, stony-faced but still

gazing into his eyes. "I want to know what happened next. Continue, please."

Bonilla hesitated for a moment and then continued to speak.

"I alerted two of the men from our column and told them to come with me. I chose a man by the name of Lorente, he being the best driver, and Miguel Doga, a courageous comrade if ever there was one, just in case we ran into problems en route. We took a car, an old Hispano-Suiza left to us by the Madrid comrades and headed for the column's headquarters in the Calle Miguel Ángel, where we knew Durruti would be. On arrival at headquarters I spotted Julio Graves, Durruti's driver, preparing the Packard they normally used ready for the road. From what they told me, Durruti and Sergeant Manzana planned a reconnaissance trip that morning. They came over when they saw us and I told them what had happened the previous night. Durruti was really angry, Major! He told me that he had a few things to say to the captain from the Del Rosal Column and would travel back with us. I went over to Julio and told him to follow us in his car because some of the streets were being raked by enemy gunfire and we would take them by the least dangerous route. They got into their car to follow us back to University City.

"Did anybody else go with them?" Fernández Durán interjected.

"No, Major. Just the three in the Packard and the three of us, Lorente, Doga and myself, up front. Nobody else was along."

"Do you know the current whereabouts of Lorente or Doga?"

"I heard tell that Doga was killed a week later in the University City, but I cannot be sure about that, one way or the other. As to Lorente, I have no idea, Major."

"And what of Durruti's usual escort?" Fernández Durán pressed again.

"He didn't come. Durruti was so pissed-off when I told him what had happened he refused even to wait for his escort. You know what a hot-head he can be..." Bonilla paused, realising his mistake... "Sorry, Major, I meant *could* be."

"Carry on," urged Fernández Durán.

"As I was saying, Major, Julio was behind the wheel of the Packard. Sergeant Manzana and Durruti were sitting in the back. Manzana's right arm was in a sling. I believe he had been injured in an accident a few days earlier. He had his *naranjero* machine-gun slung over his shoulder. We were up front, leading the way. As we approached the area where our troops were stationed, we took greater care and reduced our speed. As we turned into each street, we edged forward a little to check out the lie of the land and to allow the Packard behind us to catch up. When we turned into the last street where our billets were, we halted some twenty metres ahead to wait. Shortly after, the Packard drew up, right on the street corner. We watched as Durruti and Manzana, got out of the car to speak to five lads sitting on the pavement, smoking and sunning themselves. I can't be entirely sure, Major, but I would swear that they were from the Del Rosal column and had been involved in the attack on the Clinical Hospital the night before."

"Do you remember the exact location where they stopped, Bonilla?" asked Fernández Durán.

"To tell the truth, I don't, Major. I am a stranger in these parts and unfamiliar with Madrid. I often lose my way in these streets. That's why I brought Lorente along as driver," Bonilla replied, with an apologetic gesture. "We were near the Clinic. That I do know. In an area of chalets and low-level housing, as I have said. I think we were down towards the end of the Avenida de Pablo Iglesias, but more than that I cannot say."

"That's fine, Bonilla. Please continue."

"As I was saying, we had been parked up for a couple of minutes, waiting — glancing back every so often to check if the Packard had started to catch us up. Then, suddenly, I saw Durruti's car make a U-turn and speed back down the way we had come. I got out of the car and ran over to the *milicianos* to ask what had happened. They replied that somebody had been injured. When I asked them if they knew the occupants of the car — I was trying to worm out of them who had been wounded — their response was that they did not.

"Did you hear any shots during the time you were waiting for the Packard?" Fernandez Durán asked.

"No, Major, except for the odd, very distant report from the University area, I heard no shooting near where we were."

"Did you see any sign of a struggle between Durruti and the *milicianos* to whom he had been speaking?

"No, Major. While we were waiting I glanced back from time to time to see if they were on the move. Through the rear window of our vehicle I could see that Durruti was very angry, But I didn't know why, and I didn't see anyone making threatening gestures.

"What did you do after Durruti's car made its U-turn?"

"We made a U-turn too, and made for headquarters in case they had gone back there, but failed to find them, so we made our way back to the University City. Next day I heard from comrade Mora that Durruti had been wounded, that he had been removed to the Catalan Militias' Hospital at the Hotel Ritz — and that he had died that very morning."

Fernández Durán made no sound for a few moments, staring Bonilla directly in the eyes. The latter's edginess was growing by the second.

"Anything else to add, comrade?"

Bonilla swallowed again.

"Well, Major, it may not mean anything..." Bonilla was visibly upset. "I don't want to say anything or accuse anybody, but..."

"Out with it...", Fernández Durán cut him short.

"Two days after that we brought a wounded comrade to the Hotel Ritz where I ran into Doctor Santamaría. Mora had told me he was the doctor who had treated Durruti. I asked him what had happened, hoping to discover a little more about Durruti's final moments — and he said something very odd."

"Such as?"

Bonilla hesitated, uncertain as to whether or not he should say any more. Eventually he replied. "Among other things he told me that the shot that killed Durruti had been fired a point-blank range. He told me that he had even seen a round powder burn in Durruti's leather jacket, and that that could have only have been made by a gunshot fired at very close range."

"Do you know if Durruti was armed on the day in question?"

"He wasn't, Major. At least as far as I could see. He may have been carrying his Colt .45 inside his jacket, since he was never parted from it, but I saw no weapon on him."

"That's fine. You may go," said Fernandez Durán.

Bonilla left the room. Alcázar remained in the corner,

behind Fernández Durán who sat still, staring at where Bonilla had been sitting moments earlier. He did not utter a word. Eventually, he rose from his seat, slowly, still gazing straight ahead. He spoke, as if thinking out loud.

"Does that not strike you as odd, Alcázar?" mused Fernandez Durán, thoughtfully.

"What? Major," asked Alcázar, looking up from his notes.

"Apparently everybody knows what happened." Fernández Durán turned towards the lieutenant "They gave us all an explanation of what occurred that afternoon. What I find surprising is that everybody was happy with that explanation of things."

"I don't follow you, Major," Alcázar replied.

"It's obvious, Lieutenant. Everybody was satisfied with that explanation, everybody except us, three months on from the event and practically off our own bat and nobody wanted any further inquiries. Ever ask yourself why? Don't you get the impression that no one wants to dig deeper than the official version because maybe what they will find may not be to their liking? They all paraded their bitterness and cried out with fury at this quirk of fate — and then, what? Peace here and glory in the hereafter. This universal conformity especially rankles with me. Did you ever consider the possibility that what we were told does not fit with what happened, or rather, that they have tailored it to fit?"

"But, with all due respect, Major it strikes me that that is a desire to see something where really there is nothing. So far, the official report, forwarded by comandante Ricardo Sanz, Graves's affidavit and Bonilla's statement tally on every particular except on minor details that can be explained away by the fact that the incident occurred nearly three months ago and occasionally the memory lets one down."

"Do you believe that, Alcázar?" Fernandez Durán probed.

"Yes, Major," Alcázar replied, bewildered and startled by Fernández Durán's question.

"So, how do you account for the following, Alcázar? Bonilla tells us he went up to Graves to tell him to follow them back to University City, but Graves fails to mention this, merely saying that Durruti spoke with somebody, most likely Bonilla, and then came over to the car, informing him that they were moving out immediately for University City. In today's statement, Graves says he arrived at the Cuatro Caminos roundabout and raced along the Avenida de Pablo Iglesias at full speed. Bonilla, on the other hand, states that Durruti's car was travelling slowly behind his own — stopping every so often to check the lie of the land. Graves tells us that on reaching University City, the area was being raked by enemy gunfire, whereas Bonilla states that they ran into a group of off-duty *milicianos* sunning themselves, something that might well be partly corroborated by Graves's remark, as I recall, about it having been a splendid day. Does it strike you as reasonable that a group of *milicianos*, no matter how shattered after days of fighting, should decide to grab a little sun in an area raked by enemy gunfire? Sometimes, Alcázar, hearing is not enough; one has to listen as well. But there's more to come. According to the official report from comandante Ricardo Sanz who, remember, was not an eye witness but merely led the summary official inquiry, Manzana was wounded in the same incident that left comandante

Durruti wounded. But Graves explicitly states that Manzana already had his arm in a sling that morning. So we have confirmation from two separate sources that Manzana was wounded prior to the incident. Furthermore, it has been established that Manzana's arm was still in a sling days afterwards at Durruti's funeral. So, starting from the practically established fact that Manzana was already injured that morning, I am none too sure that Graves and Manzana, unaided — the latter with an arm in a sling — would have been able to lift a man of Durruti's bulk into the car by themselves, unless they had help from somebody else who was in the car with them that day, a fact kept from us for reasons of which I know nothing. But even skimming over this last fact, Lieutenant, Graves declared in his statement, in so many words... Let me have your notes for a moment, Alcázar... Here it is: 'I heard Durruti behind me, opening the rear door of the car and a shot rang out...' The fact that he explicitly says 'a shot' surprises me. As if picking up on one particular shot. Why does it surprise me? Because the fact that he picked up on a single shot in an area that was, according to him, being raked by enemy gunfire and constant detonations, is of itself something worth focusing on. It creates the impression that Graves picked up on that shot because there was something special about it, something that set it apart from all the rest, either because it came from a different source than the rest of the shooting, or..."

"...or because it went off very close by, plainly distinguished from the rest of the shooting to be heard in the area," Alcázar finished Fernandez Durán's sentence for him.

"And you still believe that the stories tally except for

a few trivial details, Lieutenant Alcázar?" concluded Fernández Durán with a malicious twinkle in his eye.

Alcazar was dumbfounded, not sure how to reply.

"Who's next, Lieutenant?" Fernández Durán asked.

"That leaves Captain Angulo, Major. I don't believe that Doctor Santamaría has arrived yet."

"Tell the captain to come through, Lieutenant."

Alcázar left the room, returning a few minutes later with Captain Angulo in tow. Angulo rather exaggeratedly remained standing to attention in front of Fernández Durán, as if bent on appearing as soldierly as possible.

"Captain Angulo, present and correct. At your orders, Major."

Alcázar smiled to himself. The captain's lack of stature contrasted starkly with his brio and swagger, bearing out the celebrated popular dictum '...small, but deadly.' Angulo was a career soldier of the old school, seconded by the government as military adviser to the Del Rosal Column at the start of the civil war. For him, the army was everything; it was his life and, according to his closest colleagues, he relished demonstrating this with his punctiliousness at every opportunity, even in the most mundane matters and in his dealings with other people, inside or outside of the army. He was a born serviceman and enjoyed behaving as such.

"At ease, Captain," replied Fernández Durán, beginning to sense Captain Angulo's particular character.

Angulo removed his cap and placed it with great ceremony under his arm before standing easy.

"You may sit if you prefer, Captain," Fernández Durán suggested affably.

"Thank you, Major," Angulo responded, taking a

seat.

"As I understand it," Fernández Durán opened "you were in command of one of the Del Rosal Column detachments which attempted to take the Hospital Clinic on 19 November last."

"It *did* take it, Major," replied the obviously annoyed Angulo.

"Sorry?"

"What I mean, Major, is that we did not try to take it. We captured the Clinic that same night. Regrettably, we were obliged to fall back at daybreak in the face of a fresh rebel counter-attack.

"Precisely," was Fernández Durán's answer as he tried to stifle the beginnings of a smile. "Which is to say, they took the Clinic."

"That is correct, Major."

"However, that's not why we have brought you here, Captain. Are you familiar with the events that occurred relating to comandante Durruti on the morning of the 19th in the vicinity of the Clinical Hospital?"

"Only from hearsay, Major. I wasn't around at the time."

"But there were five *milicianos* under your command who were around and whom we have found it impossible to locate. We have information that you were briefed by them about what happened. Could you tell us what your men reported to you?

"There isn't much to tell, Major. The soldiers in question were snatching a few minutes' respite..."

"As we understand it, Captain, they were falling back from the front lines," interjected Fernández Durán.

"The men under my command never withdrew unless ordered to do so, Major," snapped a wild-eyed Angulo, visibly irritated by Fernandez Durán's impertinence. "Those men were taking a break..."

"Fine. Carry on," Fernández Durán said in conciliatory tones.

"As I was saying, the men were snatching a few minutes' rest when a car pulled up alongside and two men got out of it. Apparently one of them had an injured arm that he was carrying in a sling. They approached them and the other fellow, whom we later learned was Durruti, launched into a foul-mouthed tirade, upbraiding them for hanging around, doing nothing when it was their duty to be using their guns at the front. My men did not recognise him at the time. Any more than they recognised his rank. Durruti did not like to wear emblems indicative of his rank as comandante. My men's explanation was that they were worn out firing their rifles and that for the past five days they had had no sleep, nothing hot to eat, and that he should leave them in peace. Also, that he should go and fire a few shots if he was so keen on it. Needless to say, Major, the exchange was conducted in considerably blunter language which I would rather omit from this interview.

"Understood," replied Fernández Durán. "Did your men mention whether or not Durruti or the man with him were armed?

"They told me that the man with Durruti had a rifle slung over his shoulder. Durruti himself was not carrying any visible weapon."

"The rifle. Could it have been a *naranjero*?" pressed Fernández Durán.

"They didn't mention it to me, Major. Had they done so, I would have remembered. I have excellent recall."

"Carry on with your account, Captain."

"In the end, apparently, my men told Durruti — and

I repeat they had no idea who he was — that they would be returned to the front as soon as they had had a little rest. Durruti then made his way back to his car. No sooner had Durruti opened the door and stooped to get into the car than a shot rang out. Durruti slumped, wounded. Two of my men ran over to the car and helped him inside. The car then did a U-turn and sped off like a bat out of Hell. They didn't even stop to pick up the rifle carried by the chap with his arm in a sling. It was left there in the middle of the street.

"One moment," interjected Fernández Durán. "Was Sergeant Manzana not carrying the rifle slung over his shoulder when they returned to the car?"

"Who's Sergeant Manzana?" asked Angulo.

"The man with his arm in a sling. Did he or did he not have his rifle when he got into the car?"

"According to my men, he left it behind. They picked it up and handed it in to the quarter-master."

"Do you know where that rifle is now, Captain?"

"No, Major. It was probably reissued to one of the *milicianos*. We were not exactly over-endowed with weapons."

"What happened then?"

"That same night my men heard that Durruti had been wounded in University City by a stray bullet. Suspecting this could have been the incident they had witnessed, they came to tell me what had happened, which is, in essence, what I have just recounted to you, Major."

"Where are those men now, Captain?"

"I don't know, sir. Their unit was transferred a few days later and I heard no more about them.

"Thank you for everything, Captain. I am genuinely grateful for your kindness in attending for interview.

You may go."

Angulo stood to attention before Fernández Durán.

"At your orders, Major."

Fernández Durán returned his salute and Angulo left the room.

"What do you think, Alcázar?" Fernández Durán asked, turning towards him.

"At least we seem to have discovered how they got Durruti into the car," replied Alcázar. "This version of events seems more consistent, especially when we remember Manzana had an injured arm."

"Not only that, Lieutenant. There is another significant detail," Fernandez Durán remarked, rolling his eyes knowingly.

"Which, Major?"

"Assuming Angulo's account is correct, and I have no reason to think otherwise, Manzana did not have his *naranjero* with him when he got into the car to get the wounded Durruti to the hospital at the Hotel Ritz."

"Is that significant, Major? Hardly surprising that he should have forgotten and left it behind in his haste to get Durruti into the car."

"Maybe so... or maybe not," Fernández Durán replied, pensively. "See if Doctor Santamaría has arrived yet."

"Yes, Major," Alcázar answered, sweeping out of the room.

Fernandez Durán was lost in thought. With every move they made, every interview or interrogation they held, the affair seemed to raise more questions than it provided answers. Alcázar was back in the room shortly afterwards, on his own and with a worried expression on his face.

"We have a problem, Major."

"What's going on, Alcázar?"

"I've just been told that Doctor Santamaría will not be here until tomorrow. A fresh batch of wounded has arrived at the hospital and he cannot neglect his duties.

"For God's sake!" erupted a frustrated Fernández Durán. "That's fine, Alcázar. Arrange a meeting with Doctor Santamaría for tomorrow afternoon — along with Sergeant Manzana. We can do nothing more today so the best thing is to adjourn for a rest and resume tomorrow. Just one thing. Try to find out if the rifle that Manzana normally carried was a *naranjero* or some other model. This is an important detail. Bonilla has told us that it was. If you can confirm or deny this on the basis of other sources, so much the better."

"Right away, Major."

"Off you go, but be back here tomorrow morning at ten o'clock. In the meantime I want to see for myself where the incident took place. Get some rest, Alcázar."

"You too, Major."

Fernández Durán stepped into the street. It was drizzling and the skies above Madrid were pitch black. The street was deserted except for a couple of nondescript passers-by in the distance, blurred shadows in the rain. The major turned up his jacket collar and sucked in a deep breath of damp air that worked its way right through him. He needed a breather. All night in that basement room had left him claustrophobic. After looking up at the sky, he emerged from the doorway of the Calle Fomento building and set off on foot for his room at the Hotel Atlántico on the Gran Vía (an avenue that the residents of Madrid had jokingly christened the Avenida del Quince y medio, a reference to the 4.5 inch shells with which the rebels pounded the area on a daily basis from guns positioned in the Casa de Campo). As he strolled towards the Plaza de Santo Domingo, he mentally ran through everything he had heard that evening, but could not quite arrive at any definite conclusion. All in all the facts seemed plain enough and he had no doubts as to how they had come to pass. He even agreed with Lieutenant Alcázar that all the statements seemed to corroborate them, overwhelmingly. It was the fine detail that was stymying him. The fine detail that left him, intuitively, with a sense that something did not ring true — and he was determined to ferret it out.

When he reached the Plaza de Santo Domingo and was about to make for the Plaza de Callao, Fernández Durán suddenly became aware of a tall man in a dark raincoat and hat walking behind him, keeping at a distance. This fellow had been in the doorway of the checa when Fernández Durán left and now he was tailing him. His attention had been drawn to him by that hat when he had stepped outside. In republican Madrid, such garb was poorly regarded socially and few people wore hats, these being regarded as a bourgeois accoutrement, a far cry from the cap or beret preferred by workers and *milicianos*, depending on circumstances. Fernández Durán paused in his progress and the man did likewise, keeping behind him at a distance, confirming Fernández Durán's suspicions. Smoothly, he slid his hand towards his holster, to check his gun was still where it was supposed to be; making an abrupt about-turn he strode resolutely towards his 'tail'. The stranger, caught on the hop by this unexpected turn of events, dithered momentarily then turned round and ran back down the street. Fernández Durán watched him disappear at a street junction, then resumed his trek back to the hotel, reflecting upon this curious episode. When he arrived, soaked through by the fine drizzle, he made his way to Reception to ask for his room key. He hoped to get to his room and sleep like a log that night. As he took the key, the desk clerk said to him.

"Excuse me, sir. Just one more thing. A gentleman wants to see you. He's waiting in the bar."

"For me? Are you sure?" queried a puzzled Fernández Durán. Few people were aware of his presence in Madrid and he had not been expecting to meet anybody tonight.

"Yes, sir. The gentleman was quite specific in his instructions. He told me that he needed to speak urgently with a Mr Fernández Durán as soon as he returned to the hotel."

"Thanks," replied Fernández Durán as he left the reception.

Bewildered, he made his way to the hotel bar. Although it was fairly early, the room was empty and in shadow. He spied a figure sitting alone in the far corner, a familiar face illuminated in the light cast by a lamp in the centre of the room. Fernández Durán's face showed puzzlement as he edged his way through the tables towards the man's table.

"Good evening, Major." The man greeted him, without looking up from the newspaper he was holding with two hands.

"Good evening, Minister," Fernández Durán replied, gravely. His companion closed his newspaper, folding it carefully and setting it on the table.

"Surprised to see me, Major?"

"I certainly am. No point in denying it. I thought you were in Valencia, along with the rest of the cabinet."

"Not quite, as you can see for yourself. Formally...

shall we say... officially, I am not in Madrid. I have made this trip for personal reasons. Draw up a chair, please. I decided to take advantage of my visit to call on you. I simply wanted to know how the investigation was proceeding."

"Right now, it's not proceeding anywhere Minister," replied Fernández Durán, taking a seat. "I've questioned direct and indirect witnesses to the incident and I've been examining the reports, but there are still a number of loose ends to be tied up. I'll continue taking statements tomorrow.

"And might I know your initial findings on the matter?" The minister probed with lively interest.

"It's a bit early to be talking about findings," was Fernández Durán's cautious response. "The statements hint at a few, let us say, irregular matters, just as you and the panel suspected, but it would be rushing things to draw any conclusions just yet."

"I needn't remind you, Major," the minister began in a more severe tone, visibly disappointed by Fernández Durán's reply, "that you have a duty as a soldier to abide by the orders issued to you. Your orders are clear. You must keep us abreast of everything you uncover."

"And allow me to remind you, with all due respect, Minister," replied Fernández Durán, undaunted "that I am doing my duty to the best of my ability with the resources available to me — which are certainly not particularly favourable."

"Major," the minister replied, switching to a more conciliatory tone of voice, "you were selected for this task on the basis that you are a person whom we know to be trustworthy, and of your pre-war record as a police officer. The panel has no doubts about your competency, nor does it doubt that you will do your duty."

"As you say, Minister, I was a police officer. No, it would be more accurate to say that I am a police officer," Fernández Durán declared. "The fact that I am operating in a military context is merely circumstantial. A matter of fate. I do not look down my nose at the army, but I do not regard myself as an integral part of it. I am a policeman, have been a policeman and, God willing, will be one again once this is all over. And I give you my word as a policeman, that I will do my duty with as much efficiency as I can muster."

"Rest assured, Major, that once this is all over and we have won this damned war, most likely before the year is out, your service will be handsomely rewarded and you will be returned to the job for which you seem to yearn so much. Is there anything else you need to complete this assignment? Anything: permits, appointments, interviews, passes? If there is anything you need, don't hesitate to let me know."

"At the moment, nothing, Minister. Just a couple of questions. Is there anyone else au fait with the investigation we are carrying out?" Fernández Durán asked, remembering the earlier incident of the man with the hat.

"No, Major, only the panel that commissioned you to carry out this mission. And for the moment that is how it should be. Remember, one of the conditions of your assignment was total discretion about the matter. Why do you ask?"

"No particular reason, Minister. On the other hand," Fernández Durán pressed on, changing the subject. "It would be interesting if I could get to talk to the five *milicianos* who were at the scene. Lieutenant Alcázar has tried everything to locate them, but it has proved impossible to track them down. If you could..."

"I will do all in my power to trace them. What is your schedule for tomorrow?"

"Continue with the questioning tomorrow afternoon. I am also thinking of visiting the scene of the incident tomorrow morning."

"I was just about to suggest that very thing, Major, but I can see that you are on top of things. Request a vehicle from the captain at the Fomento barracks. They have not been briefed on the nature of your assignment, but they have orders to afford you all the assistance you may need. Speaking of assistance, is Lieutenant Alcázar proving useful to you?"

"He certainly is — very efficient indeed."

"I am delighted to hear that. He's a grand lad. Anything else, Major?"

"No, sir." Fernández Durán paused, as if pondering what he was about to say and, above all, how to put it. "Apart from the event itself and how it came to pass, there is something in this whole business that has rather thrown me."

"What do you mean, Major?"

"I'm surprised at everyone's silent resignation since the incident occurred. I appreciate that the case of a man shot in combat ought not to stir up too much controversy, but right from the outset, it has been all too obvious that there are factors that do not fit, yet it took three months before anybody bothered to look into them. No one seems to care. Everybody has been too ready to accept the official version and I can't help wondering why."

"And what do you imagine the reason is, Major?"

"I can understand the government's stance. If there was a conspiracy, they should not have permitted it.

The best thing for them would be not to know for sure that they made a mistake. The people would begin to distrust those in charge of its fate. But, aside from the government's stance, it is startlingly obvious how timely the incident was, depending on the faction concerned. The communists, supported and influenced by the Russians, are at loggerheads with the anarchists because of their claim that the Party means to derail the revolution. The communists, for their part, deny the possibility of revolution to keep up the Popular Front. The incident rid the communists of a charismatic enemy who was undermining their plans. On the other hand, sections of the anarchist movement themselves were recently — and, some of them, in a very shrill way — accusing Durruti of turning Bolshevik and betraying the spirit of anarchism. The incident also rid those factions of a problem. And as for the fascists, I need not say anything about their desire to put paid to a charismatic leader like Durruti. And I don't mean in combat. You know as well as I do that right here in Madrid there are lots of cuckoos. Even in our own ranks. And no one on our side — not the government, nor the socialists, nor the anarchists, nor the communists — could feel easy about a mistake on this scale, having allowed some infiltrator to get close enough to Durruti to kill him. If that is what happened, there we have yet another reason why it might be preferable just to let the subject drop."

"The government is taking steps to get to the bottom of this matter," the minister remarked shrewdly. "The fact that we have commissioned you to carry out this investigation is one of those steps. I don't know what you are insinuating, Major, but you are on very dangerous ground. What exactly are you getting at?"

"Nothing specific. This is mere conjecture, Minister. What I mean is that, if there was a premeditated crime here, every crime is carried out because it brings someone benefit. In this case, there are lots of people who, for one reason or another, might profit from this lamentable incident. I am not accusing anyone, much less suggesting conspiracy. I am trying to get it across to you that if a murder was committed, the perpetrator or perpetrators would have a prime interest in hushing it up, but then again, people not involved in the crime might also have a considerable interest, each for a different reason, in not stirring up the matter or in looking the other way. As if everybody — whether guilty through action or omission or indeed blameless — knew for sure that something stinks here and would rather let sleeping dogs lie than have the details emerge. Forgive my bluntness, Minister, but I have serious doubts as to whether the investigation I am carrying out is wished well by the government that you represent."

The minister sat in silence for a moment, the shadow of a smile playing on his lips.

"Right. I'll detain you no longer, Major. You must be tired and you have work ahead of you tomorrow. Get in touch with me as soon as you have concluded your inquiries."

"Will do, Minister," replied Fernández Durán as he rose from his seat. "Good night."

Fernández Durán turned on his heels and made for the bar exit. He was half-way across the room when he heard the minister's voice behind him.

"See what I mean, Major? I hinted to you earlier that in my honest opinion we were right to select you to carry out this assignment."

The following morning, after a quick shower and a meagre breakfast, Fernández Durán emerged from the hotel. The day was overcast. The drizzle had stopped, but the clouds on the horizon held out the threat of rain to come. In spite of everything, it was a pleasant morning, the temperature was reasonable and a few shafts of sunlight filtered through the brooding skies above Madrid. Although he had now been in the capital for several days, Fernández Durán was still not used to the bleak picture it had to offer in those tumultuous times. He thought back to his first ever visit to Madrid before the war, when he had been pleasantly surprised by the beauty of the city. All that splendour had been marred by the madcap ideas of a band of rebel military who had brought Spain to one of the direst straits in her history.

The people of Madrid, a city where the main concern was survival, were dismal shadows of what they had been. Weary and broken, they were engaged in a daily struggle for a crust of bread, a drop of milk to prevent their children starving to death. If there was one thing that all *Madrileños* were convinced of, in those days at any rate, it was that victory over the enemy was unquestionably feasible and their current situation only a temporary difficulty. '*No pasarán!*' (They shall not pass!) was the watchword throughout Madrid. The popular wit, the classic wit so typical of Spaniards and particularly of Madrid folk, who for years had laughed at misfortune with fatalistic resignation saying '*Y si pasan, con no hablarles...*' (And if they do pass, don't speak to them...). Deep in thought, Fernández Durán made his way on foot to the nearby Calle de Fomento, arriving at a quarter to ten where he met up at the entrance with Lieutenant Alcázar. His yawns and his face signalled a sleepless night.

"Didn't you sleep well, Lieutenant?" Fernandez Durán asked.

"Oh yes, Major. I was a bit late getting to bed. I was..." Alcázar paused, "...conducting inquiries around Madrid."

Fernández Durán and Alcázar reached the interview room they had used the previous day and which doubled as a makeshift office. Fernández Durán took a seat, opened the briefcase holding the case files and Alcázar's notes from the previous afternoon, spreading the papers out on the table.

"In the wee small hours? This devotion to duty of yours will be your undoing, Lieutenant. You should learn to take things a little easier," the major retorted, amusement in his voice.

"Well, Major," volunteered a somewhat embarrassed Alcázar, "I was socialising and having a few glasses of wine with some *milicianos* from the Durruti Column. For solely professional purposes, Major." This last phrase was uttered in tones of great dignity.

"Obviously,"a grinning Fernández Durán replied. "And did you discover anything, Lieutenant?"

"Yes, Major. Several witnesses confirmed that the gun Sergeant Manzana was in the habit of carrying was of the sort described as a *naranjero*, sir."

"Interesting, Lieutenant. Very interesting. Continue."

"I also spent much of the night trying to track down anybody who might know those five *milicianos*, but nobody was able to tell me anything. It's as if the earth opened up and swallowed them, Major."

"Let us hope not, Lieutenant. Have the car brought

round. We're leaving in ten minutes. Fetch me a coffee, please, and one for yourself, if you feel like it."

"Yes, sir," Alcázar replied, leaving the room.

Fernández Durán reviewed Lieutenant Alcázar's notes. He re-read the previous day's statements from Graves, Bonilla and Captain Angulo. Alcázar returned bearing a steaming mug of coffee.

"Your coffee, Major. The car will be ready shortly."

"Thanks, Alcázar."

"Major, may I ask where we are going, precisely?"

"Good question, Alcázar. Very good question. According to the evidence from the earlier reports plus the statements taken yesterday, there are three possible locations where the incident might have happened. Because even that we are unclear about. A few accounts place it in the Plaza de la Moncloa, close to the Modelo Prison. Others have it in the middle of University City, just across from the Dental Faculty building. However, as you were able to elicit from yesterday's witnesses, there is also the claim that the whole thing happened at the far end of the Avenida de Pablo Iglesias. As I mentioned before, lots of people have jumped on the bandwagon, offering their own version of events and that has made our task more difficult. My inclination is to treat the last option rather more seriously, but we shall try to visit all the locations mentioned, as long as the rebels are not in too foul a humour today and will let us."

Alcázar smiled at his commanding officer's words, at which point the door to the room swung open and in came a captain from the unit in charge at the Fomento *checa*.

"Major, your car and escort are ready. We can leave whenever you choose."

"Escort? What escort?" queried the startled Fernández Durán. "I didn't ask for an escort. Alcázar, do you know anything about this?"

"No, Major. I made no such request either."

"Major," the captain replied, "I took the liberty of assigning you an escort party. If you intend heading for University City, that's right up on the front lines. It could be risky to go there without an escort."

"Dear God! How did this happen?" Fernández Durán retorted. "You might as well announce our arrival with an orchestra. We'll go alone, the lieutenant and I, in one car. We won't even require a driver. The lieutenant will drive."

"But Major," the embarrassed captain replied, "allow me to say that that would be rash. I would advise you to bring the escort along for safety's sake."

"I thank you for your trouble, Captain, but let me say again that not only would it be unnecessary but it would be counter-productive, since we want to keep as low a profile as possible. If our car is ready, we'll be off right now."

Fernández Durán and Alcázar left the room, heading for the street, with the captain trailing in their wake. An old black Renault was parked outside, no doubt commandeered like most of the motor pool of the Madrid militias. Behind it was parked another, similar vehicle with four armed men inside. The captain waved to the occupants of the rear vehicle, signalling their presence was not required. Alcázar climbed into the driving seat and Fernández Durán walked around the car and slid into the passenger seat. Alcázar started up the engine.

"Major," Alcázar said as they pulled out towards the Plaza de Espana, "it might be nothing, but perhaps it would have been a good idea for one of the militiamen to come with us, albeit in our own car.

Fernández Durán was staring straight ahead, deep in thought.

"Tell me, Alcázar," he asked, without turning to look. "When you requested the car, did you mention where we were going?"

"No, Major."

"So how did the captain find out where we were going?"

Alcázar hesitated before he answered.

"I don't know, sir."

"It appears, Alcázar," Fernández Durán continued "that someone is tailing us and monitoring our every move with great interest. And, given the confidentiality that we were requested to observe in our inquiries, I find it surprising that, other than the panel, there is someone else who knows where our investigations are taking us. And I suspect that yesterday, when the questioning was over, somebody tried to tail me back to the hotel, to what end I do not know."

"Did you recognise him, Major?"

"No. He took to his heels before I could get to him. I suggest that you step up your precautions from now on, Lieutenant."

"If we have to tread warily, Major, why did you not deny to the captain we were heading for University City?"

"Because there is no point denying what somebody else knows for a certainty, and the captain seemed to know already. Who told him? That I do not know. But had I denied it all that would have achieved would have been to arouse greater suspicion.

"Where to first, Major?" Alcázar asked.

"First stop, the Plaza de la Moncloa. That's the nearest point to here."

Alcázar complied with the Major's instructions. They drove past the Plaza de España and took a left turn, arriving at the ruins of the Montana barracks, mute testimony to the maelstrom visited upon Madrid in those days. They pressed on down the Calle Ferraz and, at the end of that street, turned right into the Paseo de Moret. The closer they came to the front lines, the greater the devastation around them. Virtually every building in the area was in rubble, levelled by the artillery shells from the nearby University City front. From time to time they came across a building that was unscathed, as if stoically defying death itself, but most of the homes — any that had not been reduced to heaps of smoking rubble — seemed to have been knocked to one side, gaped open or were half gone, their appearance reminiscent of so many gigantic dolls' houses, their innards open to the world. Fernández Durán reflected upon the many events, some happy, others less so, that those homes had witnesssed not so long ago. Folk had lived, suffered, loved, laughed and wept inside those walls, unaware of the end that fate held in store for them. And now that whole gamut of emotions had been reduced to next to nothing, like the walls that had hosted them. Damn this war, he thought. A thousand times damned on account of everything it had destroyed.

When they reached the Modelo Prison, Alcázar brought the car to a halt, rousing Fernández Durán from his brooding thoughts. Apart for the odd gunshot that he assumed to be coming from some way away, the area seemed quiet. In the distance he thought he could make out a group of *milicianos* moving between positions.

"According to one of the statements, this is where it happened," said Alcázar, pointing to the centre of the square. "The same statement, signed by Ramón López, states that the route taken by Durruti's car was the one we have just followed ourselves.

Fernández Durán examined the location at some length.

"I think not, Alcázar. On the basis of the statements from Graves and Bonilla which, in principle, strike me as more reliable in that they were proven eye witnesses, this route does not make a lot of sense if one is coming from the headquarters in the Calle Miguel Ángel. And both Graves and Bonilla claim to remember an area of low level housing and chalets, of which there are no sign. Then again, Lieutenant, remember that Durruti was brave but nobody's fool. I very much doubt that he would have stopped his vehicle in such an exposed area, with the front line as close as it was. Let alone that the *milicianos* he gave the dressing down to would have decided to rest up here. No, Alcázar, it didn't happen here. Let's make for the site mentioned by Bonilla and Graves. Take a roundabout route rather than pass in front of the Clinical Hospital. No point tempting fate.

Alcázar started up the car and took a right turn down the Calle de la Princesa. Within a few metres, they turned left, making for the Calle Santa Engracia. At that point, they headed for the Cuatro Caminos roundabout to cut on to the Avenida de Pablo Iglesias. They drove on until they came to the hotel mentioned by Graves and Bonilla in their statements. Alcázar drove to the end of the Avenida del Valle before bringing the car to a halt.

"This is the corner that Graves and Bonilla in their statements suggest was the location of the incident. That building over there," Fernández Durán pointed into the distance, "is the Clinical Hospital. What would you reckon the distance to be, Lieutenant?"

"Around six hundred metres as the crow flies, Major," replied Alcázar.

"That's what I reckon, Lieutenant. Well within range for a half-way competent marksman to hit his target. Let's get out of the car, Alcázar."

"That could be risky, Major," observed an apprehensive Alcázar. "We are right up in the front lines here."

"Hear any shooting, Lieutenant? The area seems quiet," Fernández Durán opined, confidently. "Although if you'd rather stay in the car, feel free."

Fernández Durán then climbed out of the car, followed, none too enthusiastically, by Alcázar. Some *milicianos* emerged from an adjacent street. On spotting them, the members of the group saluted, raising a hand to their heads and, after Fernández Durán and Alcázar returned the salute, they continued on their way towards a dirt path leading across country in the direction of University City.

"Know what lies on the far side of this green area, Alcázar?" Fernández Durán asked.

"I believe it leads directly to the faculty buildings, Major. It should come out roughly in the vicinity of the Faculty of Medicine."

"And right beside the Faculty of Medicine is the Faculty of Dentistry, right?"

"That's right, Major."

"Let's follow it for a bit. Keep your eyes peeled, Alcazar. We're on the front lines here."

Fernández Durán and Alcázar set off on foot along the path taken by the militiamen. In the distance they could hear bursts of artillery fire and the occasional isolated rifle report. The path was a quagmire. Being only a dirt track fraught with bumps and dips, the ravages caused by the recent winter downpours and artillery craters had left it impassable, to vehicles at any rate. Half-way along, Fernández Durán decided that that was far enough.

"We'll turn back, Lieutenant. I very much doubt that Durruti, if he reached the Dental Faculty as mentioned in the official report, made it through here by car. I don't think it would have been in any better condition last November than it is at present. I'm afraid we can discount the business about the Faculty."

They had just started to retrace their steps when three very short, sharp, slick whistling sounds flew past their heads.

"Damn it, Alcázar!" Fernández Durán shouted as he ducked for cover. "We're under fire! Take cover! Take cover!"

Almost simultaneously, Alcázar and Fernández Durán set off at a run, reaching a nearby foxhole about two metres across and one metre deep about half-way back, left by a shell that had landed in the area and they dived into it head-first without a moment's hesitation. Alcázar was the colour of marble. Fernández Durán's mouth was filled with a desert dryness. The very same sensation that he had heard mentioned by soldiers sent into combat for the first time. He tried to swallow some saliva, but could not. He simply had none. He popped his head slightly above the rim of the foxhole, straining to work out where the shots were coming from.

"Did you see where they were shooting from,

Alcázar?" hissed Fernández Durán.

Alcázar hesitated, looking all around.

"No, Major," replied the agitated and panting Alcázar. "I think it came from higher up, from the hospital, but can't be certain."

The area was utterly silent now. There was no one in sight, not even the *milicianos* whom they had followed down the trail. After a few minutes that seemed like hours and carefully scrutiny of the surroundings, stealing quick glances over the rim of the foxhole, Fernández Durán came to a decision.

"We have to get back to the car, Lieutenant. Keeping our heads down and moving very slowly, we will climb out of this foxhole and crawl along the ground as far as that ditch. I'll go first. Stick as close to me as you can, right?"

"Right, Major."

Slowly, the pair climbed out of the crater and crawled to the edge of the road. Time stood still. It seemed to take an eternity to reach the ditch. They paused a little after every move, muscles tensed and on the *qui vive*, waiting for the deadly shot that luckily never came. With the utmost caution, keeping their heads low to the dirt, they made it to the ditch. They dragged themselves slowly and soundlessly along the ditch until finally they reached the edge of the road, close to where they had parked the car. Half-way along two bullets thudded into the dirt close to their feet. Taking a deep breath, they jumped into the car. Alcázar turned on the ignition and they sped away.

"That was a close call, eh, Alcázar?" said Fernández Durán, sighing with relief.

"Too close, Major. Too close," replied Alcázar, still panting for breath. His heart was pounding furiously, thumping against his breast like a blacksmith's hammer on anvil.

"And we're a real mess," added Fernández Durán, looking at his mud-smeared clothes.

"Major, that incident lends weight to the enemy sniper theory. You saw how close we got. Our location was well within range of gunfire from the Clinical Hospital.

"It's one of the possibilities, Alcázar," remarked Fernández Durán. "And while we can testify as to its being a rather likely one, there are other considerations that still trouble me enough not to take that theory as read. What time are those follow-up interviews this afternoon?"

"Doctor Santamaría said that he would come around five this afternoon and Sergeant Manzana also said he would be in this afternoon, but gave no indication as to time."

"Do me a favour, Lieutenant. On the way back, drop me off at my hotel. I need to clean up and change my clothing and grab a bite to eat. You should do likewise. We'll meet up later this afternoon in the Calle Fomento."

For the remainder of the journey, Fernández Durán tried to play down the significance of the incident so as not to unsettle Lieutenant Alcázar, but, in his heart of hearts, he was convinced that they had been seriously at risk. Fifteen minutes later, Alcázar drew up outside the Hotel Atlántico, Fernández Durán got out of the vehicle and headed for the entrance. The porter, on seeing his appearance, threw him a curious look. Wearily, the major collected his room key from reception and made for his room. He slipped the key into the lock and opened the door. As he turned to shut the door behind him, something metal pressed into the back of his head and he familiar noise from his police days, a noise that froze the blood in his veins: the characteristic metallic click as a weapon was cocked for use. Fernández Durán did not move a muscle. From inside the room, he heard an unfamiliar voice:

"Please, Aranda," the voice was saying cynically. "Such discourtesy on our part! We shouldn't treat the Major this way. Take the gun away from his head, man."

Fernández Durán felt the pressure of the metal easing. He turned around slowly until he came face to face with an individual wearing a raincoat and hat; he might have removed the gun from his head, but he still had it trained on him. He instantly recognised him as the man who had tried to follow him as far as the hotel the previous night.

"Come in, come on in," the voice from the far end of the room continued. "Don't hang around the door, Major."

'Aranda' stepped to one side to let Fernandez Durán pass. With as much aplomb as he could muster, the latter walked along the hall towards the far end of the room. There, sitting on one of the armchairs, was the owner of the voice he had heard from the doorway. It was a man he did not recognise. Heavy-set, middle-aged, he wore a rather elegant, refined suit and had a thin moustache that gave him a distinguished appearance. As Fernández Durán entered, the man rose from his chair and came closer.

"Delighted to make your acquaintance at last, Major. I've heard a lot about you, a lot of good reports," the man said, holding out his hand. His movements were easy and relaxed, as if he knew that he was in control of the situation.

"I regret that I cannot say the same about yourself... Mr... ?" Fernandez Durán replied, declining to shake the hand proffered, and leaving that last word hanging in mid-air, to prompt this fellow to introduce himself.

"Pérez. Let's just leave it at Pérez," the fellow answered.

"How did you gain entry to my room?"

"In these times of scarcity, a good tip can work miracles, Major," the person styling himself Pérez replied, jocularly.

"All right, Mr Pérez. May I know to what I owe the honour?" Fernández Durán asked, straining to appear as calm as possible.

"This is a simple courtesy call, Major," Pérez replied. "I learned of your presence in Madrid and decided to stop by and welcome you.

"Damned little sign of courtesy here, Mr Pérez. I don't think holding a gun to somebody's head is among the elementary rules of polite behaviour," Fernández Durán pointed out.

"You must excuse Aranda, Major. He's a touch uncouth, but few can match him for obedience and loyalty." Pérez paused deliberately to let his next few words hit home. "What of yourself, Major? Are you a man of loyalty?"

"I pride myself upon it," Fernández Durán retorted. "At least in my dealings with those who have earned my loyalty. Loyalty cannot be bought, as seems to be the case with your man here. Like respect, loyalty is earned. In any case, Pérez, I don't think you are here to discuss moral values, are you?

Pérez said nothing for a moment. He was scrutinising Fernández Durán as if he were some

strange specimen, trying to work out the best way to broach the matter that brought him to his room. A false affable grin spread across his face.

"Even so Major. Let's get to the nitty gritty. How go your inquiries here in Madrid?"

"I don't know what you are talking about, Mr Pérez," replied Fernández Durán, imperturbably.

"Come, come, Major. Don't take me for a fool. Do you really think I am so stupid?"

"Let me say again that I don't know what you are talking about."

"Major José María Fernández Durán..." Pérez began to recite like some diligent school child who has learnt his lesson by heart. "...Born in Barcelona, orphaned at the age of three. Unmarried. No known family. Joined the Policía Gubernativa in August 1922 and, through time, rose to the rank of detective, first class. Twice decorated and specifically cited for services rendered. Chief architect of the resolution of certain difficult and outstanding crimes, including the celebrated 'bell-ringer case'. In 1930, out of the blue, he applied for a transfer to the Policía Gubernativa security corps, rising to the rank of major. In August 1936 his unit was militarised and assigned to certain guard and escort duties with various personages and organisations. Have I left anything out, Major?"

Fernández Durán looked into this fellow's eyes and noted the perverse twinkle within. His initial affability and polite manners had been replaced by extravagant, unbalanced tones and gestures which, apart from being distasteful, worried the major. The fellow faced the major's probing gaze without batting an eyelid. There was a chance that he was not quite in his right mind, but there was nothing to suggest that he was stupid.

Fernández Durán picked up on the glint of lucid madness normally seen in the eyes of many of the lowest riff-raff, and Fernández Durán had known plenty in his time. And he did appear to know an awful lot about the major. Too much for him not to appreciate that if Pérez knew the fine detail of his life and achievements, he must also be absolutely sure of the assignment that had brought him to Madrid. Fernández Durán prided himself on his ability to weigh people up and decided that this particular character was not to be trifled with. Especially when he had with him an armed man who, it appeared, was anxious to follow this Pérez's orders. The best way of handling the situation was to cut the flim-flam, and seize the bull by the horns. He made a quiet prayer that this was the right course.

"Who are you, Pérez? What exactly are you after?"

"It seems that we are beginning to understand each other, Major. Let us say that I represent the interests of certain people. Important people. People who are fervent admirers of Durruti's memory and who look upon you as sacriligious...Did I just say sacrilege? What nonsense!" Pérez said, launching into histrionic laughter. "We are republicans, after all... There is no God... As I was saying, it strikes these people as unworthy that somebody should conclude, falsely, that Durruti died other than the way he did — the way set out in the official record — thereby besmirching his memory. For reasons that need not detain us, we learned of your investigation and, believe it or not, we are here to lend you a helping hand in your assignment.

"Tell the people you say you are representing that I am grateful for their vigilance," Fernández Durán answered with studied sarcasm. "And might I ask how you intend to help me, Pérez?"

"Very simple. By expediting the onerous task that has fallen to you. Let me tell you what you are to include in your final report, the report you are to deliver to the people who entrusted this task to you. What conclusions you may have reached thus far I do not know, Major, but let me tell you that Durruti was killed by a fascist bullet. That's what happened. That's all you need to know and that's what you will set down in your report."

"And what if my findings do not agree with what you have said?"

"As I have told you already, your conclusions will be erroneous. And for your own good, I hope your findings do tally. Otherwise, it would be a great pity, Major. There would be nothing remarkable about some soldier — a major let us say — taking a bullet and dying in a heroic act of service. But you know that already. That's how capricious war can be and accidents often happen.

"Are you threatening me, Pérez?," asked Fernández Durán.

Pérez stared into the major's eyes with a cynical expression.

"I never make threats, Major. Get this. That isn't the gentlemanly thing to do. I simply like to warn others, when I have any say in the matter, about the potential consequences of their actions. I reckon we can conclude our business, Major. You must excuse me. There are other matters requiring my attention. Good afternoon."

Pérez raised his hat and, signalling to Aranda, who had said nothing during the exchange, the pair left the room. Fernández Durán's suspicions were confirmed.

Somebody else was aware of his assignment, someone whom, it seemed, was interested in upholding the official version and who was willing to resort to extreme measures in pursuit of that end; of that there could be no doubt. He suddenly became aware of his filthy, muddy appearance and decided to take that shower he so sorely needed.

After a bite to eat in the hotel restaurant, Fernández Durán set off at 4.30 p.m. for the *checa* in the Calle Fomento. His head was still turning over the curious meeting in his room a couple of hours earlier. According to his conversation with the minister the night before, there was no record of his presence in Madrid, nor of the assignment entrusted to him, yet it appeared that outsiders were aware of it. At five minutes to five o'clock, he arrived at his office in the Calle Fomento. Lieutenant Alcazar was already there. Fernández Durán decided not to mention the incident at the hotel, for the time being at least.

"Good afternoon, Alcázar," said Fernandez Durán as he took his seat. "Good afternoon, Major. Doctor Santamaría arrived five minutes ago. He's waiting in the next room."

"Show him through, Lieutenant."

Alcázar stepped out of the room, only to return within a few moments with a man in tow. The lieutenant stepped back from the door in order to let the man behind him pass through. He would have been in his thirties. Despite the weary and slightly dishevelled appearance, he was elegantly dressed and his manners were refined. Fernández Durán stood up and came over to shake the doctor's hand.

"Good afternoon. I'm Major Fernández Durán," he

said, greeting the doctor cordially. "You must be Doctor Santamaría. I'm sorry to drag you away from your duties. Would you like a coffee?"

"Yes, please," Santamaría replied. "Please excuse my appearance, but we were swamped with work at the hospital all last night and much of this morning. I haven't had more than a couple of hours' sleep."

"We shall try not to detain you unduly. Please take a chair. Alcázar, fetch the doctor a coffee."

"Yes, Major," replied Alcázar.

"What's this interview all about, Major?" Santamaría asked as Alcázar stepped out of the room.

"You shall see. We are drawing up a report on Durruti's regrettable death on 20 November last year and our information is that you were the doctor who tended him when he was admitted to the hospital. Is that the case?"

"Only partly. I was one of a team of medics, along with doctors Moya Prats and Martínez Fraile."

"But you are the official Health Chief with the Column? Is that right?"

"It is."

"And you tended to the injured man personally, right?"

"Let's say that I was the doctor who spent most time with him."

Alcázar returned to the room.

"Thank you," said Santamaría as he took the cup offered by Lieutenant Alcázar. "In any case, Major, anything I had to say, I said at the time. I still don't understand the reason for this interview."

"No special reason, Doctor Santamaría," Fernández Durán returned. "I should simply like to hear for myself what happened at the hospital once Durruti arrived there. Can you review the facts for me, please, as you remember them?"

"That's fine. I was on duty at the Confederal Militias' Hospital which, as you will know, has been set up in the Hotel Ritz. At around two that afternoon, a car raced up to the hospital with three people on board, one of them with a bullet wound in the chest. I immediately identified Durruti as the injured party. I also recognised the men with him — his driver, Julio Graves, and Sergeant José Manzana. Doctor Moya and I took charge of Durruti and we proceeded to clean and examine his injury, before he was moved to a room on the first floor. I can't remember what its number was..."

"Sorry, Doctor. These facts are already known to us," interjected Fernández Duran with as much courtesy as he could muster. "They are set out in the report. I would rather you provided me with different details than those set down in writing. Details, your own impressions. Anything, no matter how insignificant it may seem to you, could prove of value to us. Is there any detail you recall about the persons who accompanied Durruti to the hospital?"

"Such as?" Santamaría pressed him.

"Did they say anything or make any remark in your presence, or offer you any explanation of what had happened or did they speak to anybody else during their time at the hospital. Also, did the injured man say anything to you or did you see anything about the injured party to lead you to suspect anything out of the ordinary?"

Doctor Santamaría looked uneasily at Fernández Durán.

"Major, my work does not consist of passing

judgment or weighing up suspicions. My work consists of saving lives. And when I am working, I give it my full attention."

"I know, Doctor," Fernández Duran replied soothingly. "And I congratulate you for it, but any detail you might recall, however minor it might seem, could prove very useful to us."

"I remember," Santamaría reluctantly carried on (he was definitely annoyed) "that Manzana and Graves were very much on edge, something perfectly understandable in the circumstances, and that they were whispering back and forth, occasionally trading rather heated words. Shortly after delivering the wounded man into our care, they left the hospital and I did not see them again until that night, at which point they returned there. As for Durruti, as soon as we had him up in the room, we broached the possibility of an operation, not so much to remove the bullet for it was no longer there, there being an exit wound in his back, but rather to treat the internal haemorrhaging. Unable to decide, since surgery posed undue dangers, we decided to consult with Doctor Bastos Ansart, a doctor of acknowledged standing and experience. He happened to be working in the CNT Hospital in the nearby Hotel Palace. Some militiamen went off to fetch him urgently and brought him back after fifteen minutes or so. Doctor Bastos examined the injury and his diagnosis was that it was hopeless, that the injury was inevitably going to be fatal since it had passed horizontally through the upper part of the abdomen, tearing the vital organs and even affecting the pericardium, making an operation impracticable.

"Sorry, Doctor," asked Fernández Durán. "Did you say that the wound was horizontal?"

"Yes." Santamaría replied. "That was true of the entry wound — just under the left nipple — as well as of the exit wound, the middle of the back. We could argue that the trajectory followed a practically horizontal path."

"And throughout this time, was the wounded man conscious? Did he speak to you or anyone else?"

"He remained in a state of almost constant semi-consciousness. At most he mumbled two or three not very meaningful sentences. Also, to ease his pain, we injected him with a morphine solution which virtually reduced him to a jelly."

Major Fernández Durán interpreted Santamaría's pause and his subsequent response as a sign of doubt, of indecisiveness. He meant to go on probing the doctor.

"Following Doctor Bastos Ansart's diagnosis," Fernández Durán continued "you decided to await the seemingly inevitable, and the injured man was left alone with you, the sole carer. Can you remember if he said anything to you at that point?"

"I have already told you no, Major." Santamaría stated loudly, not so much edgy as irritated." Had there been anything, I have no reason to hide it."

"I'm sorry, Doctor. I didn't mean to harp on," the major apologised in a condescending voice. "Allow me one more question, please. Although weapons are not your special field, you must have seen lots of war wounds. What calibre would you say was the bullet that killed Durruti?

"I can't be certain but I would say that it was a *nueve largo*."

"One last question, Doctor. According to our inquiries, you told someone that Durruti's leather jacket had powder-burn marks, from a gunshot. A shot fired almost certainly from close range. Is that correct, Doctor?"

The doctor turned white as a sheet. His face tensed into a mask. It was quite a picture.

"I don't recall having spoken to anybody about this matter," he replied, testily. "Who told you that?"

"It doesn't matter now, Doctor," said Fernández Durán with an affable grin. "I merely wish to know if it is true or not."

The doctor made a face and answered the major reluctantly.

"Yes, Major, it is. The wounded man's leather jacket had burn marks, powder burns, which could — and I emphasis could — have been made by a shot fired from close range.

"Do you know where that jacket is now? It would be useful if we could examine it."

"I'm afraid I don't know, Major. Durruti's clothing and personal effects were picked up by members of his Column. I imagine these were handed over to the family. As to the jacket's current whereabouts, I'm afraid I have no idea."

"Thank you, Doctor, Fernández Durán concluded. "I have no more more questions. You are free to go whenever you choose."

"Thank you, Major," Santamaría replied, rising from his chair. "I hope I have been of some use to you, and I honestly hope you find what you are looking for, whatever it may be.

"I shall leave no stone unturned, Doctor. Of that you may be sure. Good afternoon."

Doctor Santamaría left the room.

"I don't know what loyalties that man is concealing, Alcázar," Fernández Durán stated, turning to the lieutenant, "but he knows more than he is telling. I'm not saying he lied to us — I honestly do not believe that he did — but given his position and, above all, his involvement in the latter stages of the incident, I am more than certain that he knows details that, for whatever reason, he was reluctant to tell us."

"That was my impression too, Major," Alcázar responded. "At one point during the interrogation it struck me his nerves got the better of him."

"Precisely, Alcázar. But let's work on the basis of what he told us, rather than what he may have hidden from us. Did you find any part of his statement interesting, Lieutenant?"

"Not especially, Major. Except that he confirmed Bonilla's remark about the jacket. I was struck by what he said about the discussion and loud whispers exchanged between Manzana and Graves, once they reached the hospital, but, apart from that, nothing."

"I've told you a thousand times, Alcázar. Listen. That's the key. One should listen and not just hear..." At this point a knock on the door, interrupted their conversation.

"Enter."

A soldier opened the door.

"Excuse me Major," the soldier said in a strained voice, "but there is a sergeant here who says he has an appointment with you. He ordered me to let you know."

"Show him in, soldier,"

A man of average height entered the room. He had a swarthy complexion with lively and expressive dark eyes, a receding hairline — and an arrogant, military air about him. He stood before Fernandez Durán, silently looking him up and down. Finally, he spoke.

"Sergeant José Manzana. You, I assume, are Major Fernández Durán."

"You assume correctly, Sergeant."

"I have no wish to appear discourteous, Major," continued Manzana, "but I have very important business to see to on the Aragon front. Matters that I have shelved in order to attend this interview. If you like, we can start as soon as possible."

"Fine, Sergeant. I shall try not to detain you long. Please take a seat."

Manzana sat down. Fernández Durán skipped the niceties and got straight to the crux of the matter.

"Were you told the reason for this interview, Sergeant?" asked Fernández Durán.

"No, sir."

"We are investigating the circumstances surrounding the death of the man who until recently was your commander-in-chief. We are interviewing everyone who was present at the time and those who, in one way or another, had knowledge of the incident. That's why you are here, Sergeant."

Manzana stared at Fernández Durán with a mixture of defiance and amusement in his eyes.

"And you reckon I have something to say about that incident that has yet to be cleared up and which is not in the official report, Major?"

Fernández Durán returned his stare, tauntingly.

"I don't know, Sergeant. That's precisely what we are here to find out."

For a brief moment Manzana continued to stare at Fernández Durán in the same arrogant manner. Then he seemed to relax, grinned and sat back in his chair.

"Exactly what is it you wish to know, Major? We received a report report that things had got a bit hairy down there, so Durruti amended his plans and decided to drop by the hospital district first. We climbed into the car and made our way there."

"Who got into the car, Sergeant?"

"Graves the driver was at the wheel. Durruti and I sat in the back seat."

"Did you make the trip alone or were you following another vehicle?"

"I don't remember. We may have been tailing the courier's car as it made the return journey. I do remember that Durruti was really angry. He had been told by the courier that that very morning they had been beaten back from the Clinical Hospital by the rebels, that our men were very demoralised and that lots of them were considering withdrawal. We were discussing all this in the car when we reached some small hotels down at the bottom end of the Avenida del Valle and spotted a group of *milicianos* who seemed to have pulled back from the front in the University City. Running into them made Durruti even more annoyed and he ordered Julio Graves to pull the car to a halt. Durruti was out of the car in a flash and dashed over to the *milicianos*. I got out after him. He ordered them to stand up and asked them what they were doing there. Needless to say they took exception to this, stating that they had been five days without food or sleep. Durruti gave them a dressing down, saying that they were not worth a crust of bread if they were letting the rebels take over Madrid, and that their duty lay on the front, that the whole of Madrid and perhaps the future of the workers of Spain hinged upon them and that they must not disappoint them. The lads, who were very young, some of them scarcely more than kids, felt ashamed and set off to walk back to the combat zone and Durruti turned back to the car.

"What happened then, Sergeant?"

"I went over and opened the rear door and, just as he was stooping to get into the car, Durruti fell to the ground like a stone, spurting blood. We could see some men positioned at the windows of the Clinical Hospital with their rifles and reckoned that one of them must have fired from his position. We then bundled him back into the car as best we could and set off immediately for the nearest hospital, the Confederal Militias hospital at the Hotel Ritz."

"Were you injured that day, Sergeant?" enquired Fernández Durán .

"Yes. I had an arm in a sling. I had an injured my right hand a few days earlier."

"Continue, Sergeant."

"We arrived at the hospital and delivered Durruti into the hands of Santamaría, the Column's senior medic. Immediately after that, we left the hospital to find Ricardo Rionda, a member of the column's War Committee, to brief him on what had happened. After we found him and briefed him, he ordered us to say nothing about the incident until such time as everything became clear and then we made our way back to the hospital looking for news of Durruti. He died early that morning.

"Were you armed that day, Sergeant?"

"Major, we were off to make a recce of the Madrid front. Of course we were armed. Durruti had his Colt and I was carrying my *naranjero*."

"A *naranjero* that you appear to have mislaid that day, correct?" Fernandez Durán asked.

For a moment Manzana's aplomb deserted him and he looked at Fernández Durán in surprise. But only for

a couple of seconds. He regained his composure immediately.

"Indeed, Major. I never found it again. I imagine that, in all the upheaval that day, I must have left it behind somewhere and never saw the damned weapon again."

Fernández Durán took a tougher line.

"Sergeant, remember that you are speaking to a superior officer and that I do not tolerate certain things," he reprimanded Manzana, harshly.

"Sorry, Major," answered Manzana, obvioulsly not meaning a word of it.

"Anything else to add to your story, Sergeant?" Fernández Durán asked.

"No, sir."

"You may go, Sergeant," said Fernández Durán, visibly troubled. "We have no further need of you for the moment, but let us know when you intend to leave Madrid."

"My plans are to leave tomorrow, late morning," answered Manzana, still seething after the major's reprimand. "Until then you can contact me at militia headquarters in the Calle Miguel Ángel. Good afternoon, Major."

Manzana picked his cap up from the table and turned to throw Fernández Durán a challenging look. Without another word, he strode out of the room, slamming the door behind him.

"Strange individual, wouldn't you say, Alcázar?"

"Yes, Major. A tough character."

"And how did Sergeant Manzana's statement strike you Alcázar?"

Alcázar hesitated. In light of his earlier misinterpretations of statements given, he had no desire to make a fool of himself again in front of the major.

"Couldn't say, Major," he began warily. "It struck me that the facts tallied in essence with the accounts of other witnesses."

Fernández Durán said nothing for a few second, lost in thought. Finally, there came the hint of a smile and he drew a deep breath, as was his wont every time he made to spell out his conclusions to Alcázar.

"Let's start with an hypothesis, Alcázar," Fernández Durán exlained. "Let's start from the highly probable fact that all the interviewees, while they may not have told us all they knew, were not lying to us in what they did say. Does that seem correct to you, Lieutenant?"

"Strikes me as a good place to start, Major."

"Right. On that basis, Graves, Bonilla, Manzana and Captain Angulo — bear in mind that the latter's evidence is not first hand, but let's accept it as valid — are agreed that Durruti was wounded as he was about to get into his car again. Right, Lieutenant?"

"That is so, Major."

"Let's focus on that key moment. The precise point at which Durruti was wounded. The point at which somebody shot Durruti."

"Agreed, Major."

"To recap," Fernández Durán went on, "Bonilla did not see the exact point where Durruti was wounded since he was in the car in front of the Durruti party and only witnessed the point at which Durruti's car did its U-turn. Julio Graves didn't see it either because he was in the driving seat and thus had his back turned, but in their statements, Manzana and Captain Angulo both — albeit that the latter's evidence is hearsay — describe that moment. Can you read me back Captain Angulo's statement on this point, Lieutenant?"

"'No sooner had Durruti opened the door and

stooped to get into the car than a shot rang out. Durruti slumped, wounded...'"

"That's fine, Lieutenant," interrupted Fernández Durán. "Now, read me back Sergeant Manzana's statement on the same matter."

"'...I...opened the rear door and, as he stooped to get into the car, Durruti fell to the ground like a stone, spurting blood...'"

"That will do for the moment, Lieutenant. Now turn to Doctor Santamaría's statement where he talks about the nature of Durruti's injury."

"Ummmmmm...Just a moment." Alcázar leafed quickly through the notes taken during the doctor's interview. "Here it is... 'That was true of the entry wound, just under the left nipple as well as of the exit wound, the middle of the back. We could argue that the trajectory followed a practically horizontal path...'"

"Now can you explain to me, Alcázar, how a shot fired, in theory, from a distance of some six hundred metres at someone stooping to enter a car causes a wound with a practically horizintal path, entering through the chest and exiting through the back? The shot would have to have been fired from below the victim, from ground level, before it could follow that trajectory through the front of someone stooping."

"A stray bullet perhaps, ricocheting off the ground, Major?"

"Possibly, Alcázar, but on the one hand, I have every reason to believe that the area was not being raked by enemy gunfire at that time. Cast your mind back to Manzana's statement. I think he said something along the lines of... 'Durruti was out of the car in a flash and dashed across to the *milicianos*. I got out after him. He ordered them to stand to attention and asked them what they were doing there'. This bears out Bonilla's statement that the *milicianos* were sitting, sunning themselves, which is hardly likely in an area swept by enemy gunfire, as I pointed out to you before, Lieutenant. Moreover, a stray shot from a *nueve largo* ricocheting off the ground and fired from a distance of roughly six hundred metres would not have enough impetus behind it to pass through a body. At best, it ought to have lodged in Durruti's body and produced no exit wound. And then bear in mind the burn mark on the jacket. There is every indicationthat the shot had to have have been fired from very close range, and from a position lower than Durruti's body, since he was stooping to get into the car."

"But, Major, on that basis , the shot could only have come from someone who was hiding beneath the car and emerged to fire at the very moment when Durruti was getting in. That's not possible."

"There may be another, simpler, explanation, Alcázar. There always is."

"I can't understand it, Major."

"That the whole thing was a ghastly accident, Alcázar," said Fernández Durán, with a wicked smirk, "but not the one they have tried to sell us."

"So what is your conclusion, Major?"

"Let's put our heads together, Alcázar. After giving the *milicianos* a dressing down, Durruti and Manzana returned to the car, right?"

"Yes, Major."

"It also seems clear that the shot was fired from close range. Doctor Santamaría appeared startled to discover we knew that detail, and, even though he could have denied it, he did not. He confirmed it, albeit reluctantly."

"That's true, sir."

"At that precise moment who were close to Durruti with weapons?"

"The five *milicianos*, Durruti himself and Sergeant Manzana. Maybe Graves, although we have no such information," replied Alcázar after a moment's reflection.

"The *milicianos* and Graves can be ruled out, Lieutenant, since the shot was fired at point-blank range. Otherwise there is no way that the powder burn mark would have appeared on the jacket.

"Sir, you're not suggesting that Durruti shot himself with his own Colt?" queried a dumbfounded Alcázar.

"No, Lieutenant. The trajectory of the bullet makes that highly unlikely. But there is still somebody left."

"Sir!" Alcázar's eyes widened.

"Tell me one thing, Alcázar? Did you notice if Sergeant Manzana favoured his right hand or his left?"

"I didn't notice, Major."

"Well I can tell you that Manzana is right-handed. I watched him pick up his cap as he left and as he reached for the door handle to let himself out. In both cases they were the actions of a right-hander. However, if he had an injured right hand on the day in question and was carrying it in a sling, over which shoulder would you say he had slung his *naranjero*?

"His left, I suppose, Major. That would be the logical answer."

"And do you think that a right-handed person can operate deftly, handling a rifle with the opposite hand to the one he normally favours?"

"Far from it, sir."

"I can't prove it, Alcázar, but I think I am pretty sure how it all happened. When Durruti came over to the car, he, or Manzana, or one of the two, opened the rear door. Durruti stooped to get into the vehicle and at that point — almost certainly at that point — Manzana's *naranjero* slipped from his left shoulder, falling to the ground and crashing to the asphalt. Remember that I repeatedly asked for confirmation that the weapon normally carried by Sergeant Manzana was a *naranjero*. I don't know if you know this, but the *naranjero* is considered one of the finest automatic weapons we have, on account of its rate of fire and sturdiness, but it is also regarded as one of the most dangerous because of its lack of a safety switch. You can try this out if you like, but, please, if you value your life, do so with an unloaded model. You only need give it a gentle tap on the ground to see how easily it fires once armed. The unfortunate Lieutenant-Colonel López-Tienda was the victim of a similar accident on the Extremdura highway barely a month before Durruti died. And let me assure you that normal practice when operating in a combat zone with a rifle is to keep it armed in case you have to use it quickly. When Manzana's *naranjero* fell and struck the ground it went off — from a lower position, as I suggested earlier, as you will see — hitting Durruti in the chest. If Durruti was bending down to get into the car at that precise moment, the likelihood is the bullet would follow a horizontal trajectory. And that was the very time when Manzana's rifle was lost. He simply left it, having forgotten it in all the confusion of the moment."

Alcázar could hardly believe what he was hearing and yet, all the pieces seemed to fit together perfectly, as in a jigsaw. Rising above his surprise, he asked:

"But, Major, if it was only an unfortunate accident right from the outset, why all the effort to cover it up?

Why not just own up to how the whole thing happened?"

"Elementary, my dear Alcázar. Everybody was eager to avoid suspicion of conspiracy. There was a lot of bad feeling around. Imagine the situation, Lieutenant. The communists are at loggerheads with the anarchists; various groups of anarchists are also at loggerheads with other groups; the Marxists of the POUM working with the anarcho-syndicalists against the communists who, with the backing of the Soviets, are trying to impose their own Russian-oriented policies. Any attempt to explain that the whole thing had been an unfortunate accident would not have been believed by any of the factions; they would have seized the opportunity to launch a tidal wave of accusations against one another that would have resulted in open warfare in the ranks of the government itself. And that would not have been to anybody's advantage. It was easier just to heap all the blame on '*a damned fascist bullet*', the fascists being the common enemy, and everybody was happy with that."

"And the government, Major?"

"The government had two main preoccupations: one, that the loss of such a charismatic leader to a silly accident would have instantly destroyed the troops' morale. Better to heap all the blame on the rebels so as to give the *milicianos* yet another reason to hate, yet another reason for fighting. And, two, explaining that the accident was down to the inadequacies of our armaments would have led, not just to loss of our own morale, but to unbelievable distrust of our war materials. The government could not and cannot admit to the fact that we are fighting with weapons that, while not all defective, are certainly unsafe and liable to

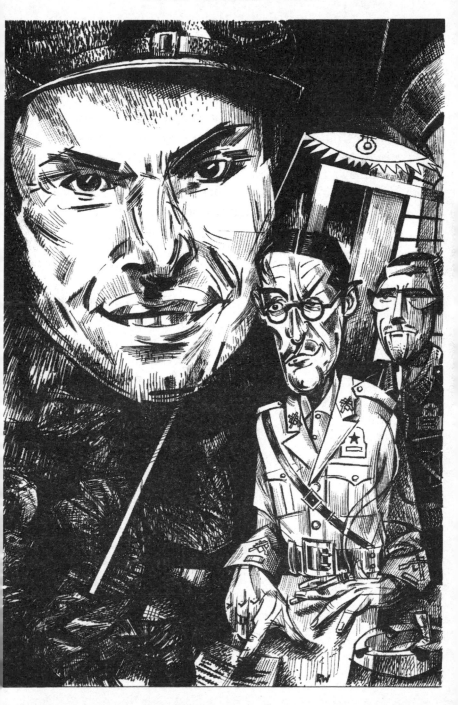

cause accidents. Have you any idea what the consequences of that would be?"

"I can imagine, Major."

"That's good, Alcázar. I will prepare my report. Contact Barcelona and tell them that our work here has been concluded. Arrange an appointment with the panel within the next three days and make whatever arrangements are necessary for us to leave for there tomorrow. You may go."

Fernández Durán stepped out of the *checa* in the Calle Fomento and headed towards his hotel. A shroud of darkness had fallen over Madrid and the sky still held out the promise of rain. He thought back to the incident in his hotel room that afternoon and checked both sides of the street. There was no one in sight. He started to trudge wearily in the direction of the Plaza de Santo Domingo, deep in his own thoughts. Although he had come to a satisfactory conclusion of the case, he could not shake off an unpleasant feeling of disappointment. In those turbulent times he was unclear as to whether or not his efforts served any real purpose. Too much politicking. Too many interests at stake. However, he felt proud that he had successfully completed his assignment. He thought wistfully of the days when he had been a policeman, a good one. He thought of all the things that the war, this damned fratricidal war that was leading Spain to ruination, had stripped from him and which he hoped some day to win back. With a bit of luck, that day might not be too far distant.

TWENTY FIVE YEARS after these events, in 1961, Major Fernández Durán was no longer a major. Nor was he even Fernández Durán. After enduring the ups and downs of the war for three long years, and indeed having personally intervened in some of the leading events of the war — and having seen the treatment meted out to his military colleagues by the victorious Francoists once the war ended — Fernandez Durán chose to disappear. Within a few weeks of the war ending Major Fernández Durán was officially reported missing and nothing more was heard of him — as Fernández Durán at any rate. For the past twenty years he had been Inspector Lobato, having returned to his former job as a policeman after going to ground for a few months at the end of the war. Following a number of tense moments and with the help his few surviving friends, he managed to reinvent himself with a new identity and, overcoming the suspicions of the new regime, he rejoined the police service.

One afternoon, he was tasked with the job of supervising security at a meeting between senior army officers and members of Franco's cabinet at a military establishment. It was a routine detail. The meeting had ended and the officers and politicians were preparing to leave and were waiting for their cars. Fernández Durán — or Lobato — was in the main hall issuing instructions to his men, ensuring that the departing VIPs left with the appropriate escort when, unexpectedly, he heard a voice from behind, addressing him:

"I know you."

Fernández Durán turned to see a short elderly army colonel accompanied by two bodyguards scrutinising him.

"Sorry?" said Fernández Durán, surprised.

"I know you," repeated the elderly officer.

"I don't think so, Colonel. Excuse me, but you must have me confused with someone else."

"No, Inspector, I do not have you confused," the colonel replied with a sly twinkle in his eye. "I have an extraordinary memory."

"Then my apologies, Colonel, but I cannot remember you."

"Can we have a word in private, Major?" the colonel asked, placing particular stress upon the last word.

Fernández Durán's heart skipped a beat.

"Certainly. Whenever you like, Colonel," he managed to reply.

"Now, perhaps?" the colonel insisted. "I will have an office prepared so we can speak in comfort. What do you think?"

"I have no problem with that, Colonel."

"Follow me, Inspector."

The colonel issued instructions to one of his escorts, ordering him to prepare an office on the upper floor and walked slowly towards the stairs. Fernández Durán followed him, warily. The colonel said nothing until, eventually, they came to an office. Standing to attention by the door was the escort who had gone ahead to prepare the room for their meeting.

"Stay by the door. I'm not to be disturbed under any circumstances," ordered the colonel to his escort, stepping inside the office. Turning to Fernández Durán he said "Please. Come with me."

The colonel closed the office door behind Fernández Durán and asked him to take a seat. The colonel looked Fernández Durán over, a slightly stunned expression on his cragged face. Fernández Durán didn't speak. Finally, the colonel opened the conversation.

"It was a welcome surprise to find you here. You have changed a lot, Major," he said tersely. "As I too must have changed, since you appear not to recognise me. Don't you remember me?"

"I'm sorry. Colonel, but let me say again that you must have me confused with somebody else. I am not, nor have I ever been, a major," replied Fernández Durán warily.

"Maybe my name will seem a little more familiar than my face. I am Colonel Angulo."

At that instant, Fernández Durán recognised the erstwhile Captain, now Colonel, Angulo. He said nothing. He decided to hold his tongue and wait. Angulo carried on talking.

"Your silence speaks volumes," Angulo pronounced, but his expression and tone of voice were affable enough. "It appears my name means more to you than my face. You are no doubt wondering what I am doing here, right? Let me dispel any doubts. A few months after our interview I defected to the Nationalists. I am a soldier and I have been a soldier all my life. I realised that my place was with my own. I knew that the republic, on account of its internal chaos, was doomed and that that was not the army I wished to serve. Shortly after my defection to the Nationalist ranks I was posted to the Ebro front where I distinguished myself in the fighting. The rest you can guess. As far as I can see, you don't appear to have done too badly for yourself either, Inspector... What name do you go by these days, Major?"

"Lobato," Fernández Durán answered laconically, his eyes remaining firmly focused on the floor.

"Lobato. So," Angulo continued. "Don't worry, Lobato. That was all a long time ago and I don't believe that anyone wishes to open old sores, least of all me. I haven't the slightest thing against the man you used to be, Lobato. You did your duty then as I did mine. And although everybody knows that I started out as a republican, I get the impression that your own past is rather less well known. Even so, I believe that we are two gentlemen and there is no point in raising issues that are of no concern to anybody else."

"Thank you for that, Colonel."

"Don't thank me. It doesn't deserve thanks. That day back in the Calle Fomento *checa* you struck me as a man of integrity. And honourable men of integrity are entitled to rebuild their lives regardless of ideology and such trifles. But I am consumed with curiosity, Lobato."

"About what, Colonel?"

"What were the conclusions of your investigation into Durruti's death? The most widely believed version these days is that a Nationalist bullet fired from the Clinical Hospital ended his life. Was that your finding, Lobato?"

"No, Colonel. I reached a different conclusion."

"Then why was it never made public, Inspector?"

"I don't know, Colonel. I handed my report with my conclusions to my superiors."

"I am afraid, Lobato, that you know only too well why your findings were not made public. In your heart of hearts you surely knew it the moment you reached your conclusions. I can guess why they were not made public, but you haven't answered my question yet. What conclusion did you reach?"

"That Durruti died from the accidental discharge of

a weapon carried by Sergeant Manzana that day, a *naranjero* that went off when it struck the ground, after slipping from his shoulder as both men were getting into the car."

Angulo was silent for a few moments, pondering Fernández Durán's words.

"Let me tell you a couple of things, Lobato. Maybe they will serve as an addendum to your report, albeit for your personal consumption only, in order to satisfy your curiosity. The first I discovered shortly after joining the Nationalist army and the other years later. Would you care for a coffee, Inspector?"

"No, thank you, Colonel."

"Right. To begin. On 19 July 1936, just one day after the glorious nationalist Rising and four months before Durruti's death, the Atarazanas barracks in Barcelona were seized by Nationalist troops who threw in their lot with the military uprising. Sergeant Manzana was one of the soldiers who supported the Rising. However, unexpectedly, the CNT, the anarcho-syndicalist labour organisation in Barcelona were prepared for the army rebellion and successfully resisted it, surrounding the military who took refuge in Atarazanas barracks. These resisters were led by, among others, Durruti and one of his group, Francisco Ascaso, a member of the CNT regional committee in Catalonia. During the battle, a well-aimed shot struck Ascaso right between the eyes, killing him instantly. Remember, Inspector, that Sergeant Manzana, was inside the barracks at this time fighting off the anarchist attack alongside other soldiers loyal to the Rising. You should also be aware that in the course of a long army career dating back to 1923, Manzana had taken part, as a soldier, in a number of national and international shooting championships and held the Master Marksman title for regulation-issue precision pistol shooting. Now, although there is no proof of any sort, either direct or circumstantal, it was one of the great quirks of fate that inside that barracks there was an Olympic standard marksman and on the outside, such a leading light of the anarcho-syndicalist movement who was cut down by such a well-aimed shot. However, be that as it may, during the confusion of the attack on the Atarazanas, Manzana defected to the *milicianos* where he quickly became an inseparable friend of Durruti's, joining his column and accompanying him through his campaigns in Aragón and Madrid, and eventually being appointed military adviser to his column. What have you to say to that, Inspector?"

"Colourful though it may be, Colonel, it all looks like sheer coincidence."

"Yes, Inspector, I know," Angulo went on. "But odd, all the same. And, taken together with other equally fortuitous circumstances it leads us down a very queer path indeed. Years later, for reasons that need not concern us here, I had occasion to read Sergeant Manzana's military record. As I said, he joined the army back in 1923, fought in the African campaigns from September 1925 until September 1926 and was awarded the Military Medal of Morocco with Larache pin and the Silver Cross for Military Merit. He passed every assessment, for conduct, valour and diligence with flying colours. Inspector, let me tell you that for a hero of Africa with a record like his to turn into an anarchist at the age of thirty five was rather unusual. Moreover, some years ago there was a rumour circulating in certain military circles — a rumour, let me stress — to the effect that Manzana was in receipt of a state pension for unknown services rendered. But the best is yet to come. Inspector," Colonel Angulo paused. "I met Sergeant Manzana."

"What are you implying?" Fernández Durán asked, stunned.

"A few years after the war ended, I saw Sergeant Manzana on one occasion. I was at a meeting in the home of a general whom I am not about to name, together with other fellow officers, when a man walked into the room. Apparently he had an appointment with the general. Spotting him as he came through the door, the general in question called out 'Here comes the man who killed Durruti'. Everyone in the room fell silent and stood stock still. The general rose from his armchair and walked with Manzana to his office where they were closeted alone for a few minutes. A few minutes later, the general emerged with Manzana, who left the room. The gathering continued without further incident and nothing more was said on the subject. No one dared make any remark. Whether or not the general made his announcement to point out Manzana as the man who killed Durruti purposely or if he was was referring to the man who killed Durruti accidentally is something I cannot determine, since I do not know the answer to that question. You must reach your own conclusion."

Fernández Durán's gaze remained fixed on the floor. He was in a daze. Angulo studied him but said nothing. Finally, Fernández Durán lifted his gaze and could think of only one thing to say.

"Thank you, Colonel," then he paused, "For everything."

"Don't thank me, Inspector. Now we shall leave by

this door. You and I do not know each other, we have never laid eyes on each other — and this conversation never took place. Understand?"

"Perfectly, Colonel."

"Inspector, I am genuinely delighted to have met you again. Adiós."

Colonel Angulo opened the door and walked out of the office. His escort snapped to attention. The elderly colonel threw Fernández Durán one last glance before joining his guards and making for the exit, leaving the major behind in the office, lost in his memories.

Alcorcón, February 2003.

Paris 14-7-1927

Despues de 13 meses de prision
y 4 dias de huelga de hambre
recobro la libertad. A causa de
sufrir por mí, los seres mas
queridos aquienes les dedico
esta fotografia con el mas
sincero cariño

Pepé

Durruti, Madrid, May 1923 (police mugshot)

ruti and Emilienne, Paris 1928

Durruti and Emilienne, Berlin 1928-1929

Leon 1915: Durruti (standing, centre) with workmates in Antonio Mije's engineering workshop

*Buenaventura Durruti was the most outstanding figure in Spanish anarchist history. Born in León of Basque and Catalan parents, on 14 July 1896, he dedicated his life from the age of 16 until his untimely death at 40 to the struggle for justice, social revolution and the anarchist idea. It was his commitment to the 'idea' that led Durruti to spend the rest of his life in clandestinity, jail, exile and — ultimately — as the inspirational figurehead of the social revolution that confronted the clerical-fascist-military uprising of July 1936.*

*Since its implantation two-thirds of a century before July 1936, thousands of militant working men and women had been prompted by the 'idea' to battle, with great resourcefulness and total dedication, and often at great personal cost, against some of the harshest social conditions in Europe. They looked forward to the autonomous cooperative commune in which all would share equally and freely the productive and administrative tasks as the basis of the just society, with the ignorance and superstition fostered by the ruling class and its allies the clergy giving way to learning, science, literature and art.*

*Towards the end of the nineteenth century, industrial unions came to be seen as the vehicles for the transition to social freedom; in their workplaces, the working class both rural and urban organised not only to defend and advance their wages and conditions but also when the time came to seize and hold the fields, factories and transport, abolish the wage system and the state, and institute an era of production to meet human needs rather than filling the pockets of the landlords and industrialists. "Comunismo libertario" (libertarian communism) was the name of this eagerly striven-for goal, poles apart in spirit and conception from the centralised, authoritarian schemes of both the parliamentarian reformist socialists and the single-party, pro-Moscow communists; the union philosophy and practice of the collective direct action that was to bring this about was called "anarcho-syndicalism".*

## MISE EN SCÈNE

BY THE 1920s AND 1930s Spain's main surviving overseas colony, held solely by means of brutal wars fought against the native peoples, was Spanish Morocco in north-west Africa. Here on 17 July 1936 the army rose in rebellion against the elected government of the Spanish republic. By the following day the long-planned rising, under the leadership of General Sanjurjo and a military directorate consisting of generals Yagüe, Queipo de Llano, Mola and Franco, had spread to the Spanish mainland.

The anarcho-syndicalist Confederación Nacional del Trabajo (National Confederation of Labour — CNT) had been preparing for the eventuality of a coup for some time. In February, just two days before the elections which were to bring to power the Popular Front government which the generals sought to overthrow, the CNT national committee in Zaragoza warned the membership of the likely backlash, should the right-wing parties be defeated in the polls. This warning was also a clear statement of intent meant for leftist Republicans and social democrats as well as for the military plotters and the landed oligarchy whose interests they served. The most powerful labour union in Spain would respond to any attempted coup with the ultimate expression of working class power — the social revolution!

Precise information as to the date of the rising had been obtained on July 13 by CNT–FAI militants in the barracks. The date was later confirmed following the arrest of a Guardia Civil officer carrying written orders. The million-plus strong CNT and its sister organisation, the Federación Anarquista Ibérica (Iberian Anarchist Federation — FAI), began to speed up their plans to resist the military and oligarchic conspiracy. In line with the February alert put out by the National Committee of the CNT, militants met frequently in their local union centres throughout Spain to prepare for the inevitable confrontation with the military.

On 16 July the CNT held a regional assembly in Catalonia to coordinate resistance plans. Arms were requested of the Generalidad (the regional government of Catalonia), but the request was rejected and CNT–FAI patrols on the streets were arrested. Censorship of the CNT newspaper *Solidaridad Obrera* prevented publication of a FAI manifesto instructing all anarchist groups to join the CNT's Defence Committees and form a united front. The text was printed as a poster and distributed illegally throughout the region.

In spite of the by now irrefutable evidence that preparations for a military coup were well advanced, neither Prime Minister Casares Quiroga nor President Lluís Companys of the Catalan Generalidad were prepared to issue arms to the only organised and reliable opposition to the military conspirators – the unions. This hesitation is hardly surprising given the clearly revolutionary nature of the country's largest labour union, the CNT. For the middle-class businessmen, civil servants and politicians of the Second Republic, the prospect of unleashing a social revolution by arming the people was more daunting than the alternative scenario of a military coup and fascism. Hoping against hope that a last minute compromise could be reached with the military, the government doggedly refused to countenance arming the people.

In Catalonia, the Generalidad had no authority over the army. Frederic Escofet, the Barcelona police commissioner, explained the dilemma:

"Arming the CNT represented a danger for the Republican regime in Catalonia – as much of a danger to its existence as the military rebellion. Could the Generalidad voluntarily adopt such measures? For my part, I believed that I could not take an initiative with such potentially serious consequences, other than trusting blindly to the triumph of the forces of public order. On which basis I was reluctant to arm the people."

"Companys and I agreed that the proper course was not to distribute the arms demanded by the people because the CNT–FAI was the dominant force. These armed elements, who would undoubtedly provide invaluable assistance in the struggle against the rebels, would also jeopardise the existence of the Republic and the government of the Generalidad. The President warned me to take especial care to guard the armouries to ensure there was no repetition of raids like those mounted on 6 October 1934. The armouries were in fact attacked the following day."

Escofet claims he did not post guards lest that distract the attentions of the security forces. He believed, however, that the government should have armed the socialist trade union, the UGT, whose leaders, for all their revolutionary rhetoric, he considered 'realistic'. Together with the forces of public order, these were perceived as being sufficient to contain the rising.

Julián Zugazagoitia, a socialist leader, quotes the following eyewitness account of Casares Quiroga's final days as premier:

> "His ministry is a madhouse and the wildest inmate is the minister himself. He neither eats nor sleeps. He shouts and screams as though possessed. His appearance is frightening, and it would not surprise me if he were to drop dead during one of his frenzied outbursts... He won't hear a word about arming the people and says in the most emphatic terms that anyone who takes it upon himself to do that will be shot."

In a last ditch attempt to stave off the military rebellion, Premier Quiroga resigned on 18 July. His place was taken by Diego Martínez Barrio, a conservative republican, who also refused to arm the workers. Martínez Barrio did everything in his power in order to reach a compromise solution with the military plotters, offering them ministerial carte blanche. General Mola, who had taken over the leadership of the revolt following the accidental death of General Sanjurjo, was offered the Ministry of War in a proposed government of national reconciliation. Mola, however, made it clear to the bourgeois republican prime minister that the class lines had been drawn up and that the political situation had reached the point of no return – confrontation was inevitable.

According to the anarchist journalist Salvador Cánovas Cervantes, Mola politely rebuffed Barrio's desperate offer in a short telephone conversation:

"I am much indebted to you, Señor Barrio, for the flattering and undeserved comments to which my work and my past service have moved you. I shall make my reply with the same courtesy and nobility you have used in speaking to me. The government with whose formation you are burdened will not get off the drawing board; should it ever take shape, it will be short lived, and, rather than remedying it, will have served to worsen the situation... You have your masses and I have mine. If you and I were to agree to some deal we should both have betrayed our ideals as well as our men. We should both deserve lynching."

As Mola predicted, the government of Martínez Barrio was short-lived, lasting only one day. In the space of three days, two governments fell rather than hand over arms to the workers. Barrio's place was taken the following day, July 19, by José Giral, who realised that all hopes of a deal were illusory. He had no option but to order weapons to be distributed to the union organisations. Giral's decree legalised what was by then a fait accompli.

On the evening of July 18, the National Committee of the CNT broadcast an appeal on Radio Madrid to mobilise for war and declared a revolutionary general strike in conjunction with the UGT. The previous day, 17 July, the transport workers' section of the CNT in Barcelona had stormed two ships anchored in the port and expropriated around 200 guns. Groups of workers raided armouries and gun shops while antique and dilapidated rifles and revolvers appeared from hiding places under floorboards and in attics. The central government in Madrid and the Generalidad which were, even at this late stage, clinging to the hope that they could reach some accommodation with the military, ordered the security forces to recover the weapons seized by the workers.

Police commissioner Federico Escofet sent a company of Assault Guards to recover the stolen arms. Guarner, the officer leading the raid on the CNT transport workers' centre where the arms were being stored, spoke to the anarcho-syndicalist militant Buenaventura Durruti who explained why the arms had been seized:

> 'There are times in life when it is impossible to carry out an order, no matter how highly placed the person who gave the order. It is through disobedience that man becomes civilised. In your case, then, civilise yourself by making common cause with the people. Uniforms mean nothing now. No other authority exists except revolutionary order, and the latter requires that these guns stay in the hands of the workers.'

Durruti's sincere speech convinced the Assault Guard captain who left with his men, taking with them a few unusable weapons, thus saving face and avoiding a confrontation. In fact, another anarcho-syndicalist activist, Juan García Oliver, turned up at Escofet's office to demand the return of these weapons. He left with four or five pistols from Escofet's drawer.

The CNT Defence Committee in Barcelona was based in the working class district of Poblenou. Two trucks had been modified for use as mobile headquarters; one was manned by the anarchists of the Nosotros affinity group, including Durruti, Francisco Ascaso, Juan García Oliver, Gregorio Jover and Aurelio

Fernández. When the CNT Defence Committee received information that the infantry regiment stationed in the Pedralbes barracks and the Montesa cavalry barracks were being mobilised, the two CNT–FAI trucks set off for their pre-arranged locations. "Workers' patrols posted along the way realised that the hour of the revolution had come." Shortly afterwards the sirens from the factories and ships in the harbour began to sound, the pre-arranged signal for the Barcelona Defence Committee to call its supporters to arms. The other mobile command post was stationed in the Mercaders Street construction union local, in the Raval area which then moved to the Casa Cambó which, was to become the "Casa CNT–FAI" when the bosses' offices were seized on 20 July. The Mercaders Street office was key to the development of the CNT Resistance Plan, drawn up before the coup."

Throughout the evening of 18 July and the early hours of 19 July, the workers busied themselves making their final preparations. When the military finally left the Pedralbes barracks at 4.15am on the morning of 19 July to occupy strategic points in Barcelona, they were met on the streets by the people in arms. Whether they were caught up in the euphoria of the moment or, perhaps, appreciated the overwhelming odds against them, first the Assault Guards and then the Guardia Civil threw in their lot with the people; then it was the turn of the soldiers on the streets to surrender their weapons.

The Sant Andreu barracks was the principle objective of the CNT Defence Committee, because of the arsenal which was to make the CNT the masters of Catalonia. The anarcho-syndicalist union had the support of the air force through Lieutenant Meana.

"I was terribly afraid of the consequences of what would happen if the arms in the Sant Andreu barracks fell into the hands of the militants – I ordered a company of the Guardia Nacional Republicana to occupy the Parque de Artillería to prevent the looting of arms there," said Escofet. Captain Francisco López Gatel was in charge — he returned shortly after with tears in his eyes and pleaded for Escofet's forgiveness for not having been able to fulfil the mission — the barracks had been invaded and the Captain had been unable to open fire on the people. "But what a responsibility for me — and how great were to be the consequences." (Escofet, *De una derrota a una victoria: 6 de octobre de 1934 — 19 de julio 1936*, Barcelona 1984, p.331).

For Escofet, the situation in the city that night was truly alarming. The rebellion had been put down but the rebels had destroyed the forces of "public order".

"Thousands of people of both sexes, who had not fought, were running through the city streets, armed and wearing combat helmets and other military clothing taken from the barracks or from the defeated soldiers; thousands of excited people, who refused to be overcome by exhaustion, did not stop celebrating — waving flags and raising the clenched fist. Civilians mingled with security guards, Assault Guards, even the CNT, unbuttoned or in shirt sleeves, raising the clenched fist, the newly minted salute of the people in arms. In those moments I asked myself with anguish how I could stem this popular tide — how could I prevent it from becoming worse?

The rebellion had been defeated throughout Catalonia. The tragic consequences provoked by the criminal elements of the military rebels became clear. The priority of the CNT–FAI was to implement the social revolution — utopian and unattainable — instead of reinforcing regimented authority. (Escofet, p.348).

"With the rebellion over I felt a need to visit President Companys in the Palacio de la Generalidad. His face showed no sign of relief at the victory we had achieved in Barcelona and throughout Catalonia over the military rebellion, a triumph which should have consolidated the authority and prestige of the Generalidad government. On the contrary, his expression profoundly grave, showing mixed emotions – sadness and worry. Possibly he saw similar emotions reflected in my face, certainly those were the ones which I felt. 'President', I told him, 'I bring official confirmation that the rebellion has been completely overcome. The last strongholds and redoubts have been taken. All the rebel chiefs and officers are prisoners. All that remains are one or two snipers.'

"'Yes, Escofet, very well,' the President replied. 'But the situation is chaotic. Armed, uncontrollable mobs are rampaging through the streets, committing every type of excess. And, on the other hand the CNT, powerfully armed, is master of the city and holds power – what can we do?'

"'President', I added, 'I undertook to bring the military revolt in Barcelona to heel, and I have done this. But authority requires the means of coercion to command obedience and these do not exist today. As a result, there is no authority. And I, my dear President, do not know how to perform miracles.' (Escofet, p.352).

"'I have spoken with General Aranguren, commander of the Guardia Nacional Republicana and also head of its four organic divisions and with General Arando, head of the Assault and Security Guards and both are convinced, as am I, that in order to restore public order, we would have to embark on a battle as great as the one we have just completed, and this simply is not possible. How can we expect our Guardias, tired but cockahoop with victory, to confront the very people with whom they have been fighting alongside for those same ideals of liberty. If we were mad enough to try it we would never succeed. For the same reason, and for reasons of humanity, the forces of public order did not fire on those who invaded the San Andrés, even though we knew we would lose all the arms. For the moment we are all at sea and that includes the leaders of the CNT. The only solution, President, is to contain the situation politically, without minimising our respective authorities – that is, if we can contain the situation politically.'"

The CNT in Madrid had also, unsuccessfully, requested weapons, and had taken matters into its own hands. A Madrid Defence Committee was set up on 18 July which organised five-man patrols, each member armed with a pistol and a grenade. According to Juan Gómez Casas, the first weapons were issued in Madrid on the night of 18-19 July on the initiative of "military personnel exasperated with the stupidity of a government that believed itself still in control of the situation." The first arms distributed to CNT and FAI workers in Madrid were those they took for themselves after storming a truck.

The focal point of the rebellion in Catalonia was the Atarazanas barracks. The Metalworkers' Union of the CNT insisted that its capture be their responsibility alone. They felt it a point of honour to avenge comrades who had fallen in the Ramblas and in the streets adjacent to the barracks. Throughout the night of the 19/20th July the libertarians fought, advancing cautiously, establishing barricades and setting up advance positions which would permit an attack on the Atarazanas barracks. Tejedor, secretary of the Metalworkers' Union, gave the following account of the attack:

> "The glorious feat of the taking of the Atarazanas was the exclusive achievement of the men of the CNT. The Guardia Civil wanted to take part in the attack but we would not permit this. It was a matter of honour... On 20 July, comrade Durruti shouted to everyone – 'Forward the men of the CNT!' Thus began the epic attack which overshadowed the capture of the Bastille by the people of Paris."

The Atarazanas fortress was not a major military target, the rebellion having been defeated, but it was a psychological success for the anarcho-syndicalists. The weapons taken from the armoury and ammunition stores provided the workers with much needed war materiel while the capture of General Manuel Goded, leader of the rising in Catalonia and the Balearics, was a major propaganda victory which seriously undermined Nationalist and bourgeois morale. The CNT's

Confederal Defence Committee of Catalonia, which had been responsible for defeating the Nationalist rising in Barcelona, refused to accept Goded's surrender. Instead they chose to press on until all the rebels had been wiped out or had surrendered. The terms of Goded's surrender, accepted by Companys, were broadcast from the Generalidad Palace. Goded's surrender, in fact, referred only to himself; he did not order the surrender of the troops under his command: "I must declare to the Spanish people that fortune has not favoured me. From this point on, any who seek to continue fighting should no longer count on me." The Confederal Defence Committee's decision to fight on after the defeat of Goded was to invest the resistance with a revolutionary depth and to shatter the myth that the working class would always be beaten by the army. Had the activists of the CNT–FAI laid down their weapons following Goded's surrender and returned home, as the bourgeois politicians no doubt hoped they would, there would have been no social revolution and the unions would have been reduced to mere auxiliaries of the forces of public order. Instead, 36 hours after the military rising started on mainland Spain, bourgeois power had collapsed and the workers, the majority of whom belonged to the anarcho-syndicalist CNT, controlled the streets of the Catalan capital and had become the de facto power in Barcelona.

Overnight, power had shifted from the smoke-filled committee rooms of the Generalidad Palace to the union locals of Barcelona. The CNT controlled arms, transport and communications. The President of the Generalidad, Lluís Companys, a remarkably astute Machiavellian politician, recognised this and immediately began manoeuvring to salvage what he could from the situation and suffocate the looming social revolution before it could get its breath back and displace the order and power structure for ever. Confident of his ability to secure the collaboration of the anarchist and anarcho-syndicalist "leadership", Companys invited CNT–FAI representatives to his office where leaders of the other bourgeois and Marxist Catalan parties had already been assembled in an adjoining room.

On behalf of the CNT, García Oliver and Buenaventura Durruti responded to Companys's call on 20 July. They came directly from the barricades as victors of the day "armed to the teeth...dishevelled and soiled by dust and smoke" to listen to the wily Companys's honeyed words. García Oliver has given the following account of what a 'visibly moved' Companys had to say:

"Above all, let me tell you that the CNT and FAI have never been treated with the respect they have deserved by virtue of their size and importance. You have always been harshly persecuted and, much to my regret, political realities dictated that I, who was once with you, later found myself with no option but to make my stand and persecute you. Today you are masters of the city and of Catalonia, because you alone have beaten the fascist military and I hope that you will not take it amiss if I remind you that the aid of the few or the many upright men of my party, of the Assault Guards and of the *Mossos d'Esquadra* was not denied you." He mused for a moment then slowly continued: "But the fact is that you, who until so recently have been harshly persecuted, have today beaten the military and the fascists. Knowing what and who you are, I can only have recourse to words of great sincerity. You have won and everything is within your power. If you have no need of me, if you do not want me as president of Catalonia, say so now, and I will be just another soldier in the antifascist struggle. If, on the other hand, you believe that I, along with the men of my party, my name and my prestige, may be of use in this office in a struggle which, while resolved today in this city is yet to be decided in the rest of Spain, then you can count on me and on my word as a man and as a politician convinced that a past of shame has today been put to rest in the sincere hope that Catalonia will put itself in the vanguard of the most socially advanced countries in the world."

The president then suggested that, under his chairmanship, the CNT–FAI, together with all the antifascist parties, should set up "an organ capable of pursuing the revolutionary struggle until victory is assured". This ad hoc ruling body was to be known as the Central Antifascist Militias Committee (CCMA). After preliminary discussions with the assembled bourgeois and Marxist politicians, García Oliver informed them that their suggestion for the Antifascist Militias' Committee was a matter for the Regional Committee of the CNT to decide and that they would be informed as soon as that body had made its determination. Companys' artful flattery and skilful manoeuvring had the desired effect. The anarchist militants who had gone into the meeting as victors emerged as the vanquished.

The following day, 21 July, the Regional Committee of the CNT hastily summoned an Extra-ordinary Assembly of Regional Plenums. According to José

Peirats, this was not, in fact, a properly constituted Plenum of Unions with an agenda to be discussed in a regular way by the union representatives; it was, rather, a gathering of militants at Regional Committee level who — attending in a personal capacity — had no mandate or authority to decide on the issues under discussion. More than a month was to pass before a regular Plenum of the Catalan CNT unions was to be held.

Mariano R. Vázquez, as Secretary of the National Committee of the CNT, gave the following account of the extraordinary and pivotal assembly in his report to the International Working Men's Association (IWMA/AIT) in December 1937:

"On 21 July, 1936, Barcelona was the venue for a Regional Plenum of the Local Federations and Sub-Regionals, called by the Regional Committee of Catalonia. The situation was analysed and it was unanimously decided not to mention Libertarian Communism until such time as we had captured that part of Spain that was in the hands of the rebels. Consequently, the Plenum resolved not to press on with totalitarian achievements, for we were facing a problem: imposing a dictatorship — wiping out all the *guardias* and activists from the political parties who had played their part in the victory over the rebels on 19 and 20 July; a dictatorship which would in any event, be crushed from without even if it succeeded within. The Plenum, with the exception of the Regional Federation of Bajo Llobregat, plumped for collaboration with the other political parties and organisations in setting up the Antifascist Militias' Committee (CCMA). On the decision of this

Plenum the CNT and the FAI sent their representatives to join it."

The Catalan middle classes were horrified by the social revolution which was gathering momentum before their eyes. Their world was being turned upside down and they shrilly denounced the anarcho-syndicalists as responsible for excesses and outrages which occurred in the wake of the workers' resistance to the military uprising. The people in arms had begun to settle old scores, directing their fury against the more notorious torturers, gunmen and professional informers of the Republic and the Dictatorship. Ramón Sales in Barcelona and Inocencio Feced in Alicante were examples of men who had been involved in the murders of hundreds of workers under the terrorist regime of Generals Martínez Anido and Arleguí from 1919 onwards and who had been summarily executed. There were also numerous cases of outrages and the settling of old scores by "eleventh-hour-revolutionists" as a means of establishing their credentials as militants.

It was the sensitive issue of "law and order" which provided the bourgeoisie with their first leverage point against the CNT. The CNT and FAI leaderships in Catalonia had shown themselves eager to establish their credentials as honourable and responsible members of the "revolutionary" government, the Central Committee of Antifascist Militias. Following a sustained disinformation campaign of exaggerated allegations, half truths and downright lies from a near-hysterical bourgeois press, offended and threatened by the close attention paid to their class by union-organised patrols and search parties, the Regional Committee and the Local Federation of CNT Unions of Barcelona rose to the bait and broadcast a warning on Radio Barcelona on

25 July, day five of the social revolution, that the CNT and FAI, as "the authentic representatives of the antifascist proletariat" had "determined upon very severe measures" which would be "enforced without a second thought" against any person or persons caught looting.

*Solidaridad Obrera*, the daily newspaper of the Catalan CNT, had, on the other hand, a more considered perspective on the alleged breakdown of "law and order".

"For a period of two days, Barcelona was reduced to two armies, each struggling to vanquish the other, and there is nothing like the stench of gunpowder to unleash all the instincts lurking in a man's soul. Then again, the upheaval reached a point where control was lost over those folk whose sole concern is the satisfaction of their selfish whims and vengeful instincts. To these and to these alone do we owe it that this week crimes (and not as many as reputed) have been perpetrated in Barcelona that the CNT and, with it, all of the organisations which have participated in the revolution, would rather not have seen perpetrated. Nonetheless, we cannot join the chorus of those who, when all is said and done, bear the responsibility, not just for the fascist revolt but also for having kept the people for years on end in a condition of permanent destitution and an even more lingering ignorance. Since these eternal grumblers have failed to do so, it is incumbent upon us to point out that looting has not been the whole story. Countless valuables unearthed during searches and in burned buildings have not wound up in anyone's private possession. The organisations of the CNT and the Antifascist Militias' Committee have in their safekeeping precious metals and objets d'art to the value of four million pesetas. The daily press has carried reports of countless instances of such items being handed over by workers who might not have a crumb to eat within the week — who can tell?"

Paying tribute to the libertarians, Police Commissioner Escofet said:

"I have to acknowledge their honesty and the romanticism of many of them who went out of their way to hand in true treasures in bank notes, valuable jewels which had fallen into their hands. Some tried to purify themselves by burning bank notes. I had to fill several safes with the goods handed in.

"In contrast, the crimes committed in Catalonia and throughout the Republican zone were generally inevitable excesses, the sort one might expect in the wake of a great revolutionary upheaval. They were disorders of the passing, ephemeral type, not part of a system based on force or the lack of humanity.' (Escofet, p.350).

The ploy of alleging excesses supposedly perpetrated against new-found partners in the struggle against fascism was successful. Not only were a number of so-called "uncontrollable" militants executed for "outrages" committed in the first weeks of the revolution, but the authority of the "higher" committees grew increasingly more powerful. It was an authority which increasingly began to target militants of their own organisation whenever they dared challenge that authority by overstepping certain limits and possibly upsetting the new found harmony in the common struggle against fascism.

The declarations and pronouncements emanating from the various committees of the CNT and FAI at this time all eschewed all reference to the social revolution which was, by that time, in full swing. Nor did they provide any guidelines. They merely confined themselves to calling off the general strike declared on 19 July, ordering a return to work and at the same time exhorting their members to press on to military victory over fascism.

The obvious unwillingness of the CNT and FAI leadership to press home their revolutionary advantage was not lost on Companys or the central government of José Giral. In the face of a massive campaign of squatting in properties abandoned by the pro-Francoist bourgeoisie, the Catalan government announced a 25% cut in rents while the Madrid government fixed the cut at 50 per cent. Instead of challenging this move by callng for socialisation of bourgeois property, which was by then a *fait accompli*, the CNT daily, *Solidaridad Obrera*, plumped for the 50 per cent rent reduction.

But in spite of García Oliver's principled opposition to collaboration with the bourgeois parties he did not refuse the nomination to serve on the Militias' committee along with Marcos Alcón, Durruti's replacement, José Asens, Aurelio Fernández and Diego Abad de Santillán. In a commemorative article on the Militias' Committee the following year, García Oliver wrote of 'the most extraordinary Plenum of Locals and Comarcals' which, summoned in haste and with delegates ignorant as to the nature of the Plenum, had succeeded in overturning the fundamental principles of the CNT:

"The CNT and the FAI opted for collaboration and democracy, eschewing the revolutionary totalitarianism which would inevitably have led to the revolution's being strangled by a confederal and anarchist dictatorship. They trusted in the word and in the person of a Catalan democrat and confirmed and supported Companys in the office of President of the Generalidad; they accepted the Militias' Committee and worked out a system of representation proportionate with numbers which, although not fair, in that the UGT and the Socialist Party, minority groups in Catalonia, were assigned an equal number of positions with the triumphant CNT and anarchists — implied a sacrifice calculated to lure dictatorially-inclined parties along the path of loyal collaboration, not to be jeopardised by suicidal competition."

In mitigation, it should be said that the overwhelming acceptance of the fateful Diego Abad de Santillán proposition by the Extra-ordinary Plenum of 21 July was not due so much to uncertain commitment to Libertarian Communism as to a conviction that a declaration of Libertarian Communism would provoke immediate international retaliation. British warships were anchored in the vicinity and, it was widely thought, preparing to land troops and occupy the city to protect British interests there. By collaborating with the bourgeois Central Antifascist Militias Committee, the CNT delegates thought they could deceive the foreign powers and the Madrid government into believing that the bourgeois democratic order still held in Catalonia while, in fact, the CNT-FAI wielded real economic, political and military power. The only people they deceived were themselves.

García Oliver claims that in spite of the overwhelming vote against the social revolution taken by the delegates at the Plenum, he still refused to accept the decision and called a meeting of the Nosotros group that same evening to propose a coup. He suggested that, under Durruti's leadership, anarchist columns should seize the main centres of government, the Generalidad and the City chambers, the Telephone Exchange and the Plaza de Cataluña, and the Ministry of the Interior and Security Directorate. Durruti, who, much to García Oliver's chagrin, had been noticeably silent during the debate, did not rise to the bait:

> "García Oliver's argument, here and during the Plenum, strikes me as splendid. His plan to carry out a coup is perfect. But this does not seem to me to be the opportune moment. My feeling is that it should be put off until after the capture of Zaragoza, which should not take more than 10 days. I insist that we shelve these plans until Zaragoza has been taken. At present, with only Catalonia as a base, we would be reduced to the most minuscule geographical area."

The Central Antifascist Militias Committee met for the first time that same night, 21 July, in the Maritime Museum where it established its permanent headquarters. Its representation consisted of the following: CNT — three; UGT — three; Esquerra Republicana (Companys' party) — three; FAI — one; Catalan Action — one; POUM — one; PSOE (Socialist Party) — one; Unión de Rabassaires (Catalan peasants' party) — one. The Generalidad was represented by a Commissioner with a military adviser. Durruti attended this first meeting as a CNT delegate, but it was to be his first and last. He felt only too keenly the contradictions and tensions existing between the rule of the Central Antifascist Militias Committee and the popular organs of the social revolution.

One of the first actions of the newly established Central Antifascist Militias Committee in Barcelona was to set about raising and co-ordinating columns from the workers' militias and armed groups which had sprung up at the instigation of the CNT Defence Committees. It was decided that the first of these columns, led by Durruti, should be sent to liberate Zaragoza which had fallen to the military under General Cabanellas. Zaragoza was an important objective, both strategically and for reasons of solidarity. It guarded the Ebro valley, dominated the entire region, was an important communications centre, and was the main obstacle to the unification of Catalonia with Asturias and the Basque country, Spain's most important industrial region. Zaragoza also had an important arsenal containing some 40,000 guns and, last but not least from the point of view of the CNT, it was an important anarchist stronghold where thousands of libertarians had fallen into the clutches of the military.

Why had such a formidable anarchist stronghold fallen so easily into the hands of the military, almost without a shot being fired? Certainly, the rising had been well organised with virtually every repressive agency of the state throwing in its lot with the insurgents. This had not been the case in Barcelona and Madrid where substantial numbers of Assault Guards and Guardia Civil had remained loyal to the Republic. The task of the military had been made easier by the government decree of July 14 which ordered the closure of all CNT locals. This had seriously limited the capacity of the anarcho-syndicalists to organise resistance, but the real reason lay elsewhere. For some time, the reformist CNT leadership in Zaragoza had been cooperating closely with the local Popular Front administration in encouraging economic recovery and collaborating with local businessmen on plans to reduce unemployment. Pronouncing in favour of voting during the February elections, they had been effectively co-opted into the system. At a meeting called by the Zaragoza CNT on the eve of the rebellion, militants had been swayed by the arguments of pacifist Miguel Abós that they should not react hastily to the military threat but should instead pursue a pacific and restrained strategy of non-violence. They had, they believed, a good working relationship with the authorities in the city and, with a membership of 30,000, thought they had little to fear. CNT militants such as Miguel Chueca and metalworker Francisco Garaita tried to galvanise resistance, but so well organised and determined were the military and their allies that by 19 July it was too late to mobilise even a fraction of the membership. The general strike called by the CNT on 19 July was, in Zaragoza, essentially a defensive rather than an offensive weapon and in the face of massive and brutal repression the strike began to weaken after a heroic two weeks of passive resistance. The only hope the workers had now lay with the militia columns from Barcelona.

MOBILISATION FOR THE attack on Zaragoza was rapid. Four days after the rebels had been defeated in Barcelona, the first militia columns began to leave the Catalan capital to liberate their comrades in Zaragoza. These working class shock troops, numbering around 3,000, had been recruited mainly from the ranks of the CNT and the FAI and were led by Buenaventura Durruti and Pérez Farrás, the column's military adviser. Other anarcho-syndicalist columns and armed groups such as that raised by Saturnino Carod, and the Ortíz column, also were hastily organised to force the rebels back and relieve the Aragonese capital.

The organisational structure of the militia units was a principal point of discussion among the volunteers. There could be no question of restoring the authoritarian militarist principles of command and obedience. Slowly, through discussion and trial and error, little by little the structure of the libertarian militias evolved as they marched towards Aragón.

In the beginning, the organisational structure was reasonably simple, evolving to meet the requirements of each new situation as it emerged. "Ten men formed a group with a delegate freely chosen to head it. Ten of these groups formed a century and the man in charge was chosen in the same way. Five centuries formed an assembly, which also had a delegate. The delegates of the centuries, and the delegate of the assembly formed the committee of the assembly. The delegates of the assembly together with the general delegate of the column formed the war committee of the column."

Durruti's military adviser, Pérez Farrás, Companys's man on the Central Antifascist Militias Committee, a professional soldier, was primarily concerned with restoring the authority of the Generalidad over the popular forces and remonstrated with Durruti over the application of libertarian principles to military organisation. Durruti replied:

> "I have already said and I repeat; all my life long I have acted as an anarchist. The mere fact that I have been given political responsibility for a human collective cannot change my convictions. It was on that understanding that I agreed to play

the role given to me by the Central Militias Committee.

"I thought — and what has happened since confirms my belief — that a working peoples' militia cannot be led according to the same rules as an army. I do think that discipline, co-ordination and the fulfillment of a plan are indispensable. But this idea can no longer be understood in the terms of the world we have just destroyed. We have new ideas. We think that solidarity among men must awaken personal responsibility which embraces discipline as an autonomous act.

"Necessity has foisted a war on us, a struggle which differs from many of those which we have waged before. But the goal of our struggle is always the triumph of the revolution. This means not only victory over the enemy, but also a radical change in man. For this change to occur, man must learn to live in freedom and develop his inner potential as a responsible individual. The worker in the factory, using his tools and directing production, is bringing about a change in himself. The fighter, like the worker, uses his gun as a tool and his acts must lead to the same goals as those of the worker.

"In the struggle, he cannot act like a soldier under orders but like a man who is conscious of what he is doing. I know it is not easy to get such a result, but what one cannot get by reason, one can never get through force. If our revolutionary army must be maintained through fear, we will have changed nothing but the colour of fear. It is only by freeing itself from fear that a free society can be built."

Shortly before leaving Barcelona for the Zaragoza front on 24 July 1936, Durruti was interviewed by Pierre van Paassen of the *Toronto Daily Star*.

Van Paassen asked him if he believed in a victory over the military insurgents to which Durruti replied that the victory would take place on the Zaragoza front. If the revolutionary forces took Zaragoza, the Northern front would be free and the revolution saved, because that was where the arsenals, munitions factories and the mines were. It also meant the revolutionary forces would control industrial Spain from Catalonia to the Basque country. The militia columns heading for Zaragoza would divide, with one column heading south to meet Franco, then advancing through Andalucía with his Foreign Legionaries and Moroccan troops. "In two, three weeks time, we will probably be fighting the decisive battles."

Van Paassen expressed his surprise, but Durruti continued:

> "Yes, a month, perhaps. This Civil War will last at least all through the month of August. The people are in arms and the army no longer counts for anything. There are two camps: civilians who fight for freedom and civilians who are rebels and fascists. All of Spain's workers know that if fascism triumphs, it will be famine and slavery. But the fascists also know what is in store for them when they are beaten. That is why the struggle is implacable and relentless. For us it is a question of crushing fascism, wiping it out and sweeping it away so that it never again raises its head in Spain. We are determined to finish with fascism once and for all. Yes, and in spite of the government."

The journalist probed further: "Why do you say in spite of the government? Is this government not fighting the fascist rebels?"

"No government in the world fights fascism to the death," replied Durruti. "When the bourgeoisie sees power slipping from its grasp, it has recourse to fascism to maintain itself. The Liberal government of Spain could have neutralised fascism long ago. Instead it temporised, and compromised, and dillied and dallied. Even now, at this moment, there are men in this government who want to go easy with the rebels. You never can tell, you know," he laughed, "the present government might yet need these rebellious forces to crush the workers' movement."

Van Paassen interjected: "But Largo Caballero and Indalecio Prieto say the Popular Front is only out to save the Republic and restore Republican order."

"That may be the view of those *señores*," replied Durruti, "We syndicalists, we are fighting for the Revolution. We know what we want. To us it means nothing that there is a Soviet Union somewhere in this world, for the sake of whose peace and tranquility the workers of Germany and China were sacrificed to fascist barbarism by Stalin. We want the revolution here in Spain, right now, not maybe after the next European war. We are giving Hitler and Mussolini far more worry today with our revolution than the whole Red Army of Russia. We are setting an example to the German and Italian working class how to deal with fascism."

"That was the man speaking," said Van Paassen, "who represents a syndicalist organisation of nearly two million members, without whose cooperation nothing can be done by the Republic, even if it is victorious over the present military-fascist revolt. I had sought to learn his views, because it is essential to know what is going on in the minds of the Spanish workers, who are doing the fighting. Durruti showed that the situation might take a direction for which few are prepared. That Moscow has no influence to speak of, on the Spanish proletariat, is a well-known fact. The most respectably conservative state in Europe is not likely to appeal much to the libertarian sentiment in Spain."

The journalist continued: "Do you expect any help from France or Britain now that Hitler and Mussolini have begun to assist the rebels?"

"I do not expect any help for a libertarian revolution from any government in the world," replied Durruti. "We expect no help, not even from our own government, in the last analysis.'

"But", interjected van Paasen, "You will be sitting on a pile of ruins."

"We have always lived in slums and holes in the wall," said Durruti. "We will know how to accommodate ourselves for a time. For, you must not forget, we can also build. It is we the workers who built these palaces and cities here in Spain and in America and everywhere. We, the workers, can build others to take their place. And better ones! We are not in the least afraid of ruins. We are going to inherit the earth; there is not the slightest doubt about that. The bourgeoisie might blast and ruin its own world before it leaves the stage of history. We carry a new world here, in our hearts. That world is growing this minute."

With Lérida (Lleida) secured, the Durruti column advanced quickly and virtually unopposed, towards Zaragoza, urging the peasants in the villages they passed through to seize and collectivise the land on which they worked. On the morning of 27 July, as the column was leaving the town of Bujaraloz, three rebel aeroplanes suddenly attacked, exposing the workers to their first major baptism of fire. The devastating blitzkrieg killed 20 men and injured many more. The men panicked. Many threw down their weapons and scattered to the four winds to escape the noise and horror of the death and destruction which rained down on them from the skies, killing and mutilating at random. When the planes had disappeared the column slowly straggled back to Bujaraloz where Durruti assembled his men in the main square to deliver what eye witnesses have described as, perhaps one of the most important speeches in his long career as an activist:

"Friends. No one was forced to come here. You chose your fate, and the fate of the first column of the CNT and the FAI is a harsh one. García Oliver said on the radio in Barcelona that we were going to Aragón to conquer Zaragoza or to lose our lives in the attempt. I repeat the same thing. Rather than retreating, we must die. Zaragoza is in the hands of the fascists. Why did we leave Barcelona if it wasn't to help them free themselves? They are waiting for us, and we start to run away. Is this how show the world and our comrades the spirit of the anarchists, by succumbing to fear when faced by three planes.

"The bourgeoisie is not going to allow us to create Libertarian Communism because we want to. The bourgeoisie will resist because it defends its privileges and interests. The only way to create Libertarian Communism is to destroy the bourgeoisie. Only then will the road to our ideal world be assured. We have left behind us peasants who have started to put into practice our ideal. They did this, feeling confident that our guns would guarantee their crops. So if we leave the road open to the enemy, it will mean that the initiatives of these peasants are useless, and what is worse, the conquerors will make them pay for their daring by murdering them. This is the meaning of the struggle, a thankless one which resembles none that we have undertaken before. What happened today is a simple warning. Now the struggle is really going to start. They will shoot at us with cannons. They will strafe us with tons of grapeshot and sometimes we will have to fight with grenades, and even with knives. As the enemy feels cornered, he will respond like a beast and will bite fiercely. But he isn't yet at bay and is fighting to avoid this. He counts on the aid of Italy and Germany. If we allow these powers to become deeply involved in our war, it will be difficult to beat the fascists because they will have armaments superior to ours.

"Our victory depends on the speed with which we act. The faster we attack, the greater chance we have of winning. Up to now victory has been ours. For that reason we must conquer Zaragoza at once. Tomorrow we will not have the same chances as today. In the ranks of the CNT there are no cowards and the men of the FAI may die, but they do not yield. We don't want people among us who are afraid of the first attack. I ask those who ran, hindering the advance of the column, to have the courage to drop their weapons so that firmer hands can pick them up. The rest of us will continue our march. We will reach the North. We will join hands with our Asturian comrades and we will conquer and give Spain a better prospect. I ask those who go back to keep silent about what happened today because it fills me with shame."

The attack at Bujaraloz was a bitter but invaluable lesson which helped turn a raw body of inexperienced men into an army of fearless warriors. But the march on Zaragoza was halted. The officer in charge of the Barbastro garrison, Colonel Villalba, and Pérez Farrás the military adviser seconded to Durruti, pressurised the anarchist not to advance further until his flanks had been secured. There was also a problem of a shortage of weapons and ammunition. Also, the Central Antifascist Militias Committee (CAMC) in Barcelona had decided, in its wisdom, that Majorca was of greater strategic importance than the capture of Zaragoza and refused to issue the column with the necessary weapons and ammunition required to advance the 35 kilometres to the Aragón capital.

The fateful halt outside Zaragoza lasted nine days, during which time the initiative passed to the insurgents. The unexpected breathing space enabled the military and their rightist supporters to break the general strike in Zaragoza, an anarcho-syndicalist stronghold, by slaughtering the leading working class militants.

Durruti went immediately to Barcelona to press the case for the attack on Zaragoza and to stress his column's urgent need for war material, but the CAMC had decided that the social revolution was to be subordinated to the contingencies of the war against fascism. According to the professional military advisers 'seconded' to the militia columns by the bourgeois Generalidad government, the attack on Majorca took precedence. Their argument was that taking Majorca would force an Italian intervention which, in turn, would lead to direct intervention by Britain to restore 'the balance of power' in the Mediterranean. Zaragoza was abandoned to its fate, the anarchist and revolutionary militias were prevented from taking control of northern Spain, and the social revolution received its first strategic setback.

Durruti was to become an increasingly painful thorn in the side of the bourgeois politicians and of the leadership of his own anarcho-syndicalist union, the CNT. He was convinced that the only way to win the war was by prosecuting the libertarian revolution which had prevented a successful military coup in the early hours of 19 July. To Durruti and many other anarchists, war and revolution were inseparable; only a libertarian revolution could finally destroy fascism — because doing so meant destroying the state, since fascism was only a particular mode of the state; all states turn fascist when privilege is threatened.

The decree militarising the militias was published on 20 October and had been hotly debated within the Durruti Column itself, which had decided not to accept it, in that it did not hold out any prospects of improving the fighting capabilities of the *milicianos* who had volunteered on 19 July, nor did it offer a solution to the chronic shortage of arms. The Column also rejected the need for a barrack-style discipline and argued that revolutionary discipline was superior to it: "*Milicianos* yes, soldiers never".

Interviewed by the French anarchist paper *L'Espagne*

*Antifasciste*, Durruti openly criticised the proposed militarisation:

> "...This decision by the government has had a deplorable effect. It is absolutely devoid of any sense of reality. There is an irreconcilable contrast between that mentality and that of the militias ... We know that one of these attitudes has to vanish in the face of the other one. "

November 1936 proved a milestone in the civil war. Having surrounded Madrid, the mutinous army made a supreme effort to over-run the capital. On 4 November 1936 the leadership of the anarcho-syndicalist CNT agreed to join the central government of Largo Caballero. Many believed that this was a cynical move on the part of Caballero to facilitate the government's flight to Valencia and to pre-empt any criticism, or, presumably, any revolutionary initiatives from the anarchist rank and file. Indeed, two days later, on 6 November, Largo Caballero and his cabinet, including his newly appointed anarchist ministers, fled to Valencia while the people of Madrid rallied to the city's defence to cries of 'Long Live Madrid Without Government!'

Under strong pressure from Federica Montseny acting on behalf of the Council of Ministers, Durruti, increasingly dismayed about the steady erosion of the gains of the social revolution in the rearguard while militants were sacrificing their lives daily, reluctantly agreed to broadcast an appeal for militia volunteers to save Madrid.

Durruti's appeal was broadcast on CNT-FAI radio on 4 November. As Column delegate, he used his speech to spell out the sense of indignation and betrayal felt by *milicianos* on the Aragón front at the plainly counterrevolutionary turn of events and developments behind the lines.

Durruti's broadcast began at 9.30 pm. It contained not one word of demagoguery or rhetoric in the entire speech. They were hard, harsh, words for those at the top — and for those at the bottom, the workers, and for the CNT hierarchs. It was a diatribe against bureaucratisation of the revolution and an indictment of the government's policy, whether CNT personnel were in it or not. Durruti was making it clear that this was not a fight for any Republic or bourgeois democracy, but a fight to see the social revolution succeed and the people emancipated:

"Workers of Catalonia: I address these words to the Catalan people, the selfless people who, four months ago, lowered the boom on the military goons who sought to ride roughshod over them. I bring you greetings from your brothers and comrades fighting on the Aragon front. They are within kilometres of Zaragoza and in sight of the towers of the Pilarica.

"Despite the threat looming over Madrid, we should keep it in mind that we are a risen people and that nothing in this world is going to make us back down. We shall hold out on the Aragón front against the Aragonese fascist hordes and we turn to our comrades in Madrid to tell them to hold out, for the *milicianos* of Catalonia will do their duty — just as they took to the streets of Barcelona to crush fascism. The workers' organisations must be mindful of their over-riding duty at the present time. On the front lines as well as in the trenches, there is but one thought, a single aim. Eyes are fixed, looking ever forward to the sole aim of crushing fascism.

"We ask the people of Catalonia to have done with intrigue and internecine strife: prove yourselves equal to the circumstances; set aside all rancour and focus on the war. The people of Catalonia has a duty to match the efforts of those fighting on the front. There is nothing for it but for everyone to mobilise. And it must not be thought that it is always the same people who should be mobilising. While Catalonia's workers must shoulder the responsibility of serving on the front, the time has come to require sacrifice from the Catalan people living in the cities too. We need an effective mobilisation of all workers in the rearguard, because those of us already at the front want to know the calibre of the men we have at our backs.

"Let me address the organisations and ask them to cease their squabbling and intrigues. Those of us at the front require honesty of them, especially from the CNT and the FAI. We ask the leaders to act with honesty. It is not enough for them to send us letters at the front egging us on and for them to send us clothing, food and ammunition and rifles. They too must prove equal to the circumstances and look to the future. This war boasts all of the drawbacks of modern warfare and is costing Catalonia dearly. Leaders must take it on board that if this war drags on, a start must be made to the organising of Catalonia's economy and on a code of conduct in economic affairs. I am not prepared to scribble more letters just to secure an extra crust of bread or glass of milk for the comrades or children of a militiaman while there are ministers who can eat and drink their fill. We turn to the CNT-FAI to tell them that if they, as an organisation, control the economy, they should be organising it properly. And let no one think right now about wage rises and cuts in working hours. All workers, especially CNT workers, have a duty to make sacrifices and work for as long as it may take.

"If we truly are fighting for something better, the *milicianos* who blush when they read in the press of the donations raised for them and when they see the posters asking for aid for them will prove it to you. Fascist planes fly over us, dropping newspapers in which we can read of subscriptions raised for their fighters, the very same as ourselves. So we have to tell you that we are not beggars and do not accept charity in any form. Fascism stands for and is, in effect, social inequality. Unless you want those of us who are fighting to confound those in the rearguard with our enemies, do your duty.

"If you would make provision against that danger, you should form a granite block. Politics is the art of chicanery, the art of living the high life, drone-like, and this must give way to the art of toil. The time has come to invite the trade union organisations and political parties to have done with this once and for all. There must be proper administration in the rearguard. Those of us at the front want to feel that there is responsibility and reassurance at our backs and we insist that our organisations look out for our wives and our children.

"If the militarisation decreed by the Generalidad is meant to scare us and foist an iron discipline upon us, you are sadly mistaken. You are mistaken, Ministers, with the decree militarising the militias. Since you prattle about iron discipline, I say to you: come with me to the front lines. We who are there do not accept any discipline because we have enough conscience to do our duty. And you will see our order and our organisation. Then we shall go down to Barcelona and ask you about your discipline, your order and your control, which are non-existent.

"Rest easy. There is no chaos and no indiscipline on the front. We are all responsible, and we know the prize you have entrusted to us. Sleep soundly. But we left Catalonia entrusting the economy to your care. Take responsibility and show discipline yourselves. Let us not, through our incompetence, spark a further civil war in our own ranks after this war.

"If there is anyone thinking that his party may be in a better position to impose its policy, he is mistaken, because fascist tyranny can only be resisted by means of a single force and there should be only one organisation with a single discipline. There is no way in this world that these fascist tyrants are going to get past us. That is the watchword here at the front. To them, we say: 'You shall not pass!' And it is up to you to chorus: 'They shall not pass!'"

Durruti left Aragón with about 1,000 volunteers and made his way through Lérida (Lleida), Barcelona, Valencia and then on to Madrid. Federica Montseny's insistence that Durruti and 1,000 of his men should come to Madrid, which already had 200,000 defenders, prompted García Oliver, an old comrade of Durruti, to ask if she 'wanted to kill Durruti.' At the Bakunin barracks in Barcelona, Durruti gave another memorable speech to his comrades in arms:

> "Do you want to come with me to Madrid, yes or no? It is a question of life or death for us all. We will either conquer or die, because defeat will be so terrible that we could not survive it. But we will conquer. I have faith in our victory. I only regret that I speak to you today in a barracks. Some day barracks will be abolished and we will live in a free society."

Durruti gave such a description of a society without injustice and cruelty that most of the men who were listening cried. As García Oliver recalled: "when at the end he asked the question again: 'Are you coming with me, yes or no?' it was such a unanimous 'Yes,' so sincere and so deep that I can never forget it."

By the time Durruti and his volunteers arrived at the Vallecas barricades on the outskirts of the besieged capital on 14 November his column had swollen to around 1,800 *milicianos*."

The defence of Madrid was bloody and it was vicious. It lasted from 7 November until 20 November. On his arrival on the evening of 14 November, Durruti was given responsibility for a sector of the University campus where another column, the Libertad-López-Tienda, commanded by a certain 'Negus' of the PSUC (the Catalan Stalinist party), was also posted. At dawn the following day, 15 November, both the Durruti and Libertad-López-Tienda columns launched a frontal assault in an attempt to prevent Franco's Moorish troops from crossing the Manzanares river. The pressure was too great. Fresh Nationalist reinforcements under General Asensio managed to force their way into the School of Architecture, having wiped out most of the Libertad-López-Tienda Column and around a third of Durruti's men.

On 17 November, German Junkers aircraft began their intensive blitzkrieg bombing raids wreaking death and destruction throughout the city. That day Durruti wrote what were to be his last words:

"I have come from the land of Aragón to win this fight which today is a question of life or death, not merely for the Spanish proletariat but for the world as a whole. Everything hinges upon Madrid and I will not attempt to disguise my delight at finding myself face to face with the enemy, if only because it lends nobility to the struggle. Before taking my leave of Catalonia, I asked that those involved in the struggle be conscientious. I am not referring to the poor in spirit or those who are lacking in vigour. I mean those of us committed to pressing onwards, ever onwards. Rifles are of no avail if there is no determination, no ingenuity in their use. There is no question of the fascists entering Madrid, but they must be repulsed soon, for Spain must be retaken. I am happy in Madrid, I make no bones about that; it delights me to see her now with the composure of the serious minded man who is alive to his responsibility and not the frivolity and bewilderment displayed by a man when the torment looms."

Just after midday on 19 November, Durruti, accompanied by his driver Julio Graves, Miguel Yoldi, Antonio Bonilla and his military adviser Sergeant

Sergeant Manzana (left), Mora (daughter of Francisco Ferrer Guardia); Buenaventura Durruti (right)

Manzana, set out for the Clinical Hospital, the scene of serious fighting with Moorish troops. Spotting a group of *milicianos* he thought were deserters, Durruti stopped the car and got out to order them to return to their positions, which they did. As he opened the car door to re-enter, a burst of machine gun fire from inside hit Durruti in the chest at point blank range. According to Miguel Yoldi and Sergeant Manzana, the bullets came from Durruti's own machine gun when it accidentally knocked against the car door. According to the third occupant of the car, Bonilla, however, the fatal shots were fired 'deliberately or accidentally', by Sergeant Manzana. According to García Oliver, Durruti never carried a machine gun, only a pistol. Buenaventura Durruti, the 'troublesome priest' of anarchism, died from his wounds in the early hours of November 20, aged 40 years.

Not entirely convinced that Durruti's death was the accident or the work of a sniper as represented by the National Committee of the CNT, and worried that Madrid was a trap designed to eliminate the anarcho-syndicalist militants, what remained of the Durruti Column wanted to leave the Capital immediately. Only the hurried arrival of Federica Montseny managed to persuade them to remain in Madrid. García Oliver, in spite of the personal doubts he claims to have harboured about Durruti's death, had no faith in the capacity of the rank and file to accept the circumstances of the death at face value and judge for themselves. It was he who took it upon himself to release the manipulative lie that Buenaventura Durruti had died as a hero at the hands of an unknown sniper.

On 21 November, the National Committee of the CNT and the Peninsular Committee of the FAI issued the following statement:

> "Workers! The snipers of what has come to be known as the "fifth column" have floated the fallacious rumour that our comrade Durruti has been vilely murdered by an act of treachery. We caution all comrades against this foul slander. It is a squalid ploy designed to smash the proletariat's redoubtable unity of action and thought [which is] the most efficacious weapon against fascism. Comrades! Durruti did not perish through any act of treachery. He fell in the fray, as have so many others fighters for freedom. He died a hero's death: while carrying out his duty. Let us be unanimous in rejecting this despicable innuendo devised by fascists for the purpose of smashing our indestructible unity. Reject it without euphemism and in its entirety. Pay no heed to mavericks peddling fratricidal rumours. They are the revolution's greatest enemy!"

Durruti's body was taken by car to Barcelona where the funeral took place on 23 November. It was one of the most important working class demonstrations in the history of the Spanish labour movement, with over half a million people lining the streets of the Catalan capital to pay their respects to an indomitable working class hero. This was the biggest public display of grief in Barcelona's history. Durruti was laid to rest beside his closest comrade, Francisco Ascaso, who had died in the assault on the Atarazanas barracks four months earlier, and an earlier anarchist victim of vicious state repression, Francisco Ferrer Guardia.

But they had to kill Durruti twice. On the anniversary of his death, the lie machine of Moscow's puppet Spanish premier, Negrín, went into overdrive to credit Durruti with coining a phrase that had been devised originally by the Soviet writer Ilya Ehrenburg in a doctored interview with Durruti and which had then been backed by the CNT-FAI's higher committees. Durruti had allegedly said, "We renounce everything except victory," which in fact was the exact opposite of everything he had always said and thought, because it foreswore the revolution.

Unfortunately, there is no complete and reliable transcript of Durruti's 4 November speech, because the anarchist press at the time both sweetened and censored the living Durruti. However, CNT historian José Peirats was present at the very meeting at which the 'official' CNT press later claimed that Durruti had effectively reneged upon the revolution in favour of the war, and his extensive notes revealed that no such declaration had been made. Peirats concluded that the words imputed to Durruti were part of a cynical fabrication by those who then controlled the CNT propaganda machine to exploit the prestige of one of the anarchist movement's most charismatic figures in order to pursue its own political and strategic objectives during the war (see

Chris Ealham's introduction to *The CNT in the Spanish Revolution*, Vol 1).

Once dead, Durruti could be deified. He was even promoted, posthumously, to the rank of Lieutenant-Colonel in the Popular Army, a rank he would never have accepted in life. An uncompromising anarchist and intransigent revolutionary, Durruti understood how power damaged both those who commanded and those who obeyed, and shunned every organisational position and formal military rank, as well as all honours and awards during the Civil War.

Command of the Durruti Column passed to Sergeant Manzana and Miguel Yoldi, both of whom would play crucial roles in imposing militarisation on the column.

Durruti's death on 20 November 1936 signalled the beginning of the end for the libertarian revolution that

Durruti's funeral: (left to right) Enrique Perez Farras (Durruti's military adviser); Manuel Mora Torres, Commander of the 16th Division (Army of the Ebro), linking arms with Sergeant José Manzana who, in turn is holding the arm of Durruti's partner, Mimi (Emilienne Morin).

LA VANGUARDIA

Entierro de Buenaventura Durruti

had begun so hopefully on 19 July 1936. By the end of May 1937, seven months later, the social revolution in Catalonia, the Levante and Castile had been forcibly extinguished, and by the middle of August that year troops of the 11th Division commanded by the Stalinist General Enrique Líster had dismantled the agrarian collectives of the Council of Aragón at bayonet point. With them fell the last beacon of libertarian

communism. Ironically, the events of May in Barcelona and August in Aragón triggered the final collapse of Republican Spain. The complete disintegration of the front lines in March 1939 emphasised the profound effect that the disarming of the militias and moral devastation of the rearguard had had on the people's will to resist.

Making imaginative and ingenious use of the literary device of the detective novel, Pedro de Paz has explored various hypotheses and interests that could at last provide us, seventy years on, with believable answers to the many questions as to the chain of events that led to the death of a truly remarkable man. To speculate on what might have been had Durruti not been shot that November day is pointless. There were many who benefited from his death — or at least breathed a sigh of relief on hearing the news. But if it wasn't the result of an accident it is useful to consider why a man of his moral and ethical stature could not be allowed to live, providing as he did a charismatic focal point for the libertarian aspirations of the Spanish working people. By every account of the thousands who knew and admired him for his many gifts, Durruti was an inspiration in thought, word and deed, and had he survived to live even into his early-middle forties he undoubtedly would have continued to be a clear and present obstacle to the agendas of the myriad interest groups contending for political power and influence in Republican and Nationalist Spain.

Stuart Christie

Barcelona police commissioner, Federico Escofet

**Durruti,** Madrid, November 1936

Durruti with a group of milicianos on the Aragón front

(Top) Bujaraloz, October 1936: Durruti with his partner Emilienne, also part of the Durruti Column
(Below) Bujaraloz, November 1936: Durruti informs the column that they are needed to defend Madrid

Durruti's funeral procession from the *Casa de la CNT*, Barcelona 23 November 1936

Chief mourners: Manuel Mora, Sergeant Manzana, Emilienne Morin, Luisa Satnamaria (wife of Miguel Yoldi), Francisca Subirats

(Below) Montjuic cemetery, Barcelona, 23 November 1936: Durruti is laid to rest beside Francisco Ascaso and Francisco Ferrer Guardia. Juan Garcia Oliver is in the centre, and on his left Juan José Domenech, secretary of the Catalan regional Committee of the CNT. The speaker is CNT-FAI press secretary Bernardo Pou.

Contribuid pro-monumento a
# DURRUTI
y a todos los heroes caidos en la lucha

Entregas: Reforma Agraria, 20.-Madrid